One More Night

Rebecca Hunter

CONTENTS

1   Temptation   1

2   Seduction   47

3   Warning   125

4   Redemption   207

5   Epilogue   273

TEMPTATION

1

FOR MY FIRST trip to a foreign country, I was doing well. Of course, I had spent the day working in English, so that wasn't too much of a challenge. But now, I was testing my luck at the pub. An Irish pub, hopefully increasing the chances of a wait staff that understood me. If not…well, I'd figure something out. I had been so hungry I'd left the hotel without even bothering to blow out my hair, and every time I turned my head, the red, springy curls bounced into view. But tonight, it didn't matter. Stockholm wasn't New York.

I signaled the bartender.

"English?" I called over the din.

He wrinkled his brow, then nodded. "Yes."

"A burger and a glass of red wine, please?"

The creases in his brow grew deeper. I waited, but the bartender just stared at me.

I tried again. "A burger and a glass of wine, please?"

He nodded and turned away. Hmm. Did that mean *I'll order that right away* or *I give up*?

Leaving the fate of my dinner in the bartender's hands, I scanned the room for a reasonably private booth. I planned to get some reading done over dinner, but if the pub was already this loud at six in the evening, the likelihood of working seemed slim. Maybe the mini-bar in the hotel room would have to do.

I slid into the last booth along the windows, away from the noise of the television. I pulled out the stack of manuscript excerpts I had picked up at the Stockholm Book Expo and flipped through the pages. There it was. The latest by the elusive Jonas Hällström.

I stared at the cover page and frowned. He was supposed to be at the event in person. My face flushed. I had even lingered at his publisher's table, assuming the author of a truckload of bestselling dark thrillers would actually show up. But he didn't.

I slipped his manuscript to the bottom of the pile. Where was my wine?

I looked across the pub for the bartender and froze. A guy was staring right at me. His hands were shoved in his pockets, emphasizing his broad, thick shoulders, the kind that belonged in a gym or a boxing ring. He gazed at me, wide-eyed, as if he was surprised to see me. As if we knew each other. But that was impossible. I knew no one on this side of the Atlantic. So why did he look so familiar?

3

The guy started across the room, his hands still stuffed deep in his jeans pockets. Hints of tattoos peeked out from under the sleeves of his white t-shirt, and his whole body radiated *fuck you.* Everything except those eyes.

He stopped in front of my table, but he didn't say anything. His eyes were even more intense close up. Bright blue with long, dark lashes and laugh lines that crinkled the corners. Wide and full of surprise. Neither of us moved. His gaze fell to my lips, my throat, pausing as if he were committing me to memory. I couldn't look away. I took a deep breath, inhaling the warm scent of his body.

"Do I know you?" I finally asked, breaking the spell.

"Sorry." He stepped back a little.

I blinked and let my gaze fall to his thick biceps and muscular forearms. The kind I would never let myself come close to back in New York. But here he was, close enough to touch.

"I didn't mean to startle you," he murmured. "You just look like…"

A crease formed between his eyebrows, and his deep blue eyes searched mine. I waited for the end of his sentence, but it never came.

And now I was staring at him.

"Nice to meet you, whoever you are," I said, straightening up.

That earned me a smile. "I'm Jonas."

4

He reached out a large, warm hand, scarred at the knuckles. I tried not to stare. I really did. He couldn't feel my pulse thumping in a handshake, could he? His accent was a mix of Swedish and something else—Irish? And his voice was low and husky, like he had already smoked a lifetime's worth of cigarettes.

Wait. Was this...? The grainy photo on the back of his books didn't do him justice. He was a lot bigger, especially up close.

"Jonas Hällström?"

He froze. His eyes darted across my face for a moment before he relaxed.

"Yes," he said slowly. "I'm surprised you recognized me."

I swallowed and tucked a rebellious lock of hair behind my ear. For ten years I had succeeded in being the kind of woman who didn't look twice at a guy like Jonas. A guy with sexy, dark eyes and a deep voice who looked like he could beat the crap out of anyone in the room. Shit. Apparently, I still hadn't rid myself of my taste for dangerous men.

But I was in Stockholm. No danger in getting hung up on the wrong kind of guy when I was leaving the country tomorrow. I could just talk to him. Nothing more.

"I'm Alice," I said in my practiced business voice.

The corners of his mouth turned up.

"I know who you are, too," he said. "Alice O'Connor, Acquisitions at Boars and Allen Publishers. You picked up my manuscript today."

Oh. Of course. He wasn't actually flirting with me. This was about his book. But my heart pounded wildly at the way he said my name—*Ah*-leez. And the way he had stared at me just minutes ago had nothing to do with business... did it? The heat tingled at the base of my neck. Damn. I was blushing. I brushed a few wild curls off my face. Of course I had left my hair ties behind.

"Can I sit?" he asked.

This was my chance to say no. To end it all right here.

"Yes, of course," I said.

I expected him to sit on the opposite side of the booth, but instead he slid in next to me until his leg rested against mine. And he smelled good. No, good wasn't the word. Delicious. He was newly showered, and I inhaled a whiff of his faint aftershave before I could think better of it. My heart pounded double-time. He rested his arms on the table, and I tried not to stare. Really, I tried.

"I didn't see you at the book expo today." Definitely not. I wouldn't have missed a guy like this.

"I was there, practicing my charm, as my publisher likes to say." He gave a wry smile.

"And now you're about to try it on me?"

"I already am. Can't you tell?" Those intense blue eyes sparkled.

"I'm overwhelmed." I let out a little laugh. "What's the book about?"

"Nothing you'd be interested in." He ran his hand through his hair, and for a moment, his smile faltered.

I raised an eyebrow. "How do you know what I'm interested in?"

Jonas's eyes widened, and he looked at me carefully.

"I don't," he said softly.

He kept his gaze fixed on me, and I was no longer sure we were talking about his book. Another warm flush crept up the back of my neck. This guy gave off a kind of wild energy that had no place in the sterile, florescent-lit book expo.

Sometime during this conversation, he had moved closer again. I drew in a breath. What was I doing?

Nothing I couldn't walk away from.

Jonas cleared his throat and straightened up. "But my book has turned out to be what you American publishers call unmarketable."

"Sweden has a population of nine million people, and the U.S. has 300 million," I said. "If the book found a market in Sweden, why not in the U.S. as well? The numbers are on your side."

He chuckled. "I like the way you think." Slowly, his smile faded until he was looking at me so intensely I had to look away.

"You're not what I expected," I said softly.

He let out a long breath. "So, Alice O'Connor, what are you doing here without anything to eat or drink?"

I shrugged. "I don't know. I thought I ordered something, but maybe you need to teach me some Swedish? I thought I'd have better success with my English at an Irish pub, but I guess not."

The corners of his mouth turned up. "I can go get you a beer."

I frowned. "I don't like beer."

"What kind of American doesn't like beer?"

I rolled my eyes. "This kind. 300 million people, remember?"

"Got it," he said. "What would you like?"

"I ordered a glass of red wine, but I can get it myself," I said.

He looked at me carefully. "Alice, I'd really like to get your wine. I have dinner here a couple times a week, so I'm pretty sure I can communicate with the guy behind the bar."

How could I say no to that? I started to thank him, but when I met his gaze, I stilled. In his eyes was a silent question, though I had no idea what that question was. Or maybe I did.

"What do you want to eat?"

"A hamburger," I said in what I hoped was some semblance of a normal voice.

He nodded. "I'll be right back."

He slid out of the booth and walked over to the bar. Instinctively, I put my hand up to my hair. Why hadn't I blown it straight? After my quick get-yourself-together shower, it was probably a frizzy mess. I took a deep breath.

Forget the hair. Just talk about his story. And think about snow. And ice.

But I lost any gains in cooling my thoughts as soon as Jonas sat down next to me again. He pushed a glass of wine in front of me and took a sip of what looked like water.

"Thanks. Nothing for you?" I asked, my voice throaty and suggestive. Damn.

His eyes widened, filling with heat. Then he shook his head. "Not tonight."

I sipped my wine, hoping to tame some of my fluster. His leg rested against mine again, but I didn't move away. Why wasn't I giving this man my well-practiced frostiness right now? I had honed these skills back in high school, when I was still tempted by guys like this.

I swallowed and turned to Jonas.

"Aside from the fact that you live nearby, what are you doing here? Have I stumbled onto Stockholm's secret writer hang-out?"

Jonas shook his head. "I saw you through the window."

I bit me lip. He was studying me again, and he wasn't shy at all about staring. Each time I met that gaze, it was hard to remember what I wanted to say.

"Why did you want to talk to me?" I finally asked.

He leaned back in the booth, the amused grin returning. "There's no good way for me to answer that, is there?"

"What do you mean?"

"Well, I can tell you what you think I'm doing here," he said. "You think I'm sitting here to somehow win favor for my book, to convince you by less than noble means to take it back to your boss and sell it to him. And if I said that to you, you'd believe me, but that would be the end of this conversation."

Jonas kept his eyes fixed on me as he spoke. He rested his arm on the table and turned to lean closer. His full lips were only inches from mine, soft and inviting. I drew in a quick breath. This guy certainly was sure of himself.

"But if I told you the truth, you might run, too. For different reasons." He sighed, but his mouth quirked up. "We'll find out soon enough."

I could barely concentrate on what he was saying. When he spoke, his voice, seductive and low, spread through my body, awakening it. Was he playing with me? I turned my head to hear him over the noise of the pub, avoiding his gaze. His hand grazed my cheek as he set a strand of my hair free from behind my ear.

"When I saw you this morning, I had to meet you," he said, his voice a whisper now. "But by the time I got to the table, you were gone."

His dark eyes sparkled. He had seen me at the Stockholm Book Expo. Noticed me.

"Now I get a second chance to use the charm I was working on," he said, leaning back, his voice now casual again. "And it may be my last chance. You're probably not in Stockholm for long."

I shook my head slowly. "I'm leaving tomorrow for Denmark."

"Ah, well..." His voice drifted off, and he took another sip of his water. "That's not much time. But I think I can work with it."

I sat up a little straighter. "What do you have in mind?"

Jonas let out a low, rumbling chuckle that sent a rush through me. "I'm not sure how to answer that."

My face burned again. It must be the accent. His sexy mix of Irish and Swedish made everything he said sound just a little dirty. What was I interested in? Before I could think better of it, my gaze wandered to his soft, full lips and the thin scar along his jaw. He didn't get a scar like that from writing.

"You're pretty intense," I said. "You know that?"

Jonas chuckled. "I've heard that before. It's all or nothing."

"But it seems to work well for you."

"Sometimes." Jonas sighed. "Certainly helps with the writing. But it's gotten me into a lot of trouble, too."

I'd been right. It had taken me only seconds to figure out that he was trouble, and now he had confirmed it. But I was leaving tomorrow, so did it matter? Maybe. Before I could ask what kind of trouble, the bartender came by with two burgers. He slid them forward and said a few, incomprehensible words to Jonas before returning to the bar.

Jonas turned to me. "I got one with cheese and one without. Just in case."

"Without, please," I said.

He set one of the burgers in front of me and turned his attention back to his own. Now I was grateful he sat next to me instead of across the table so I could eat unwatched. Between bites, I snuck glances at him instead. Sitting next to him, he looked even bigger. All that don't *fuck with me* muscle was impossible not to notice. My body hummed with awareness of his thick thigh brushing up against mine. His knuckles bore the kinds of scars that were all too familiar. I had seen the kinds of fights that gave scars in my old neighborhood. But there was something different about him, too. Unlike the guys from my neighborhood who fought, he wasn't restless. He seemed perfectly content to quietly eat next to me.

He finished first and turned to the game on the TV, letting me finish my burger in peace. A couple guys passed by and nodded to Jonas, and he nodded back, but his eyes were harder, colder.

I took my last bite and pushed away my plate. I tucked an unruly lock of hair behind my ear and searched for something safe to talk about. But the same question nagged at me: Why was I still sitting here with him?

No good answers came, so I grabbed the pile of manuscripts on the table and lifted his from the bottom. He turned back to me, and his expression softened.

"So you're Jonas Hällström, author of a bunch of very successful thrillers," I said. "And now you've written an unmarketable book. I'm intrigued."

Jonas took a deep breath and frowned a little. He crossed his arms and looked right at me, all flirtation gone. "I'll give you the very short version. It's the story of a relationship between a Swedish man and a red-headed American woman, but it's dark, with lots of sex."

I narrowed my eyes. "Are you making this up?"

"What makes you ask?" Some of the seriousness from his expression faded.

The corners of my mouth turned up. *Was* he joking?

"Okay," I said, "international relationship, dark, lots of sex—doesn't sound hopelessly unmarketable to me."

He raised an eyebrow. "That's what my publisher thought, too. But, apparently, if a novel about a destructive relationship with dark sex is by a woman, it's considered romance. The same kind of story written by a man is misogynistic porn."

I gave a little snort of laughter. Hopefully it sounded light. Hopefully it hid the catch in my breath at the words *dark sex*. Damn. That curiosity was supposed to be buried long ago. What I really needed to focus on was the *destructive relationship* part of that sentence.

Wait, he was talking about his book, not him, right? Or maybe not. My heart pounded harder.

My smile faded as I met his gaze. He was looking at me intently, studying everything I did. He was letting me know he liked what he saw. And I liked what I saw, too. A lot. If I was leaving for Copenhagen tomorrow, did it matter what came next? Maybe I could just give it a try. Something I could never, ever do back in New York.

I leafed through the first pages of his manuscript, stalling.

I stopped, my eyes fixed on three words in the middle of the page: *curly red hair*. The American woman in his dark story with lots of sex had curly red hair. He didn't make that up.

"So now you see why I wanted to talk to you this morning," he said softly. "But this part I didn't count on." He gestured around at the pub, and then he smiled. "Your straight hair from this morning is even curly now."

I closed my eyes. At that moment, I was my old self back in Brooklyn, not the woman I had worked so hard to become. That other version of myself. I wanted just a little more taste of it.

I took a deep breath and opened my eyes. Jonas was still watching me, his eyes dark and suggestive. Who did he see when he looked at me?

My own question from earlier came back: What was I interested in? I still didn't have an answer.

I looked down at the manuscript, skimming through the pages. More phrases jumped out at me: … *she hitched up her skirt and straddled him…she knelt down in front of him and licked her lips…*

Shit. I had never once straddled my ex-boyfriend or knelt down in front of him and licked my lips, not even in the beginning. Jonas, on the other hand, looked like the kind of guy who had been straddled more than his fair share of times.

"You know, I'm not the woman in your book," I said.

Jonas nodded slowly. "I know. And I'm not the man in it, either. Not anymore."

He fingered a few of my loose curls, letting his hand brush over my shoulder. A trail of goose bumps ran down my arm. What would his large, warm hands feel like on my bare skin? I wanted to know the answer.

He leaned forward and whispered in my ear, "But we all have many sides, sides that we don't always let show, don't we?"

I closed my eyes and swallowed hard. Oh, God. Just once I could be the kind of woman who would straddle this man. Who would kneel down in front of him. Who would make a man with a *don't fuck with me* body want something badly.

And Stockholm was probably the best place to do it. Because I knew no one. Because with a bank account like mine, I was probably never coming back.

I opened my eyes. Jonas had turned to look into the crowd that now filled the bar, two-people deep. The room was filled with the din of men's voices, cheering for the soccer game on the TV screen and calling out to each other. One guy shoved another, but it ended in laughter.

He rested his arms against the table and took a sip of his drink.

"Does it get rowdy in here?" I asked.

Jonas frowned. "Mostly just on the weekends." He gestured to the TV screen. "But tonight's a big game. You'll be fine."

Because I was with him. He didn't have to say the words. He slid closer to me, his big, muscular thigh pressed against mine, his body between me and the crowd.

What was it like to be Jonas, to move through the world knowing he could take on anyone? I looked down at the scarred knuckles as he lifted his glass. Not an easy life. He'd done more than just intimidate.

Guys who had knuckles like that huddled in groups on my old Brooklyn street, blocking the way to school. Their arms were decorated with tattoos, too, usually with some mixture of religion and soft porn. They could show a girl a good time for a night. That was never a question.

But they never, ever became writers. So who *was* Jonas Hällström, with his scarred knuckles and his hard muscles and a couple dozen books under his belt?

He set his glass down. I would have expected a guy like him to have finished about three beers by now. I drifted my fingers over his hand before I realized what I was doing. I quickly pulled my hand back.

"Sorry."

Jonas smiled. "Don't stop on my account."

His deep blue eyes were open and welcoming, and he seemed to be waiting for my next move. I buried my hand under the table. Probably better just to ask my questions rather than make more stupid moves while I thought about them.

"How did you become a writer?" I asked.

It was the most basic question, but his expression hardened. He turned away.

"Never mind," I said, looking down into my glass.

He shook his head, and when he turned back to me, I saw a glimpse of something. Regret?

He ran the back of his hand over the bare skin of my arm, sending a delicious shiver through me. I turned to him, and he brought his hand up to my face. He caressed my cheek with the kind of gentleness I never would have expected from a man like him. Or maybe I didn't know what kind of man he was after all.

"If you really want to know the answer, I'll tell you," he said softly. "You can look it up anytime. But I'd rather not talk about it. Not tonight."

I leaned into his touch. "There isn't anything more than tonight."

"Perhaps."

I waited, but he was silent again. His thumb stroked my jaw, and his expression softened.

"What can I ask?"

Jonas shrugged. "What else do you want to know?"

Where did I start? I had a hundred questions about his past. All of them would probably bring back the same wariness in his eyes. Or maybe even the stony gaze he gave the other men in the pub.

His warm hand moved to my shoulder, and he rested it there. My body hummed with the slow caress of his fingers. He was still watching me, waiting.

I met his gaze, straight on. "If you could go anywhere, where would it be?"

"To live or to visit?"

"Either."

"There are a lot of reasons I wouldn't move from Stockholm, but to visit?" He closed his eyes, and the corners of his mouth turned up into a smile. "If I had my way, we'd be in Paris right now."

We. Not just him. What else did he imagine us doing together?

"What about you?" he asked. "Where do you want to go?"

I shrugged. "Paris sounds good to me. I'd go anywhere outside the US." I paused. "You know, this is my first trip out of the country. I never even owned a passport before a couple weeks ago."

"All the more reason to go," he said quietly.

Had the discussion shifted past just imagining? I and my ex-boyfriend had never traveled further than New Jersey together, but Jonas looked serious. I frowned. There was no reason to get excited about something that would never happen.

A deep crease formed between his brow, and he pulled his warm hand away.

"I don't want to scare you," he said, backing up. "I just came over here to sit with you for a while. Talk."

My frown grew deeper. He was backing down now? He had broken off the intimacy of the moment, and he looked like he was ready to walk away.

It was now or never. If I ever wanted a taste of the kind of guy I had sworn off, this was my chance. The danger didn't come the first night. With a guy like this, the really good parts came first. Until a girl was hooked. Then the destructive parts came out.

Before better judgment could intervene, I blurted out, "What if I want more?"

He stilled, and his eyes grew darker. "Do you?"

I swallowed and nodded. I leaned forward and brushed my lips against his. He let out a soft groan, so I did it again. I caught his lip and the new stubble of his beard, a mix of soft and rough. He rested his warm hand on my cheek and pulled back. His eyes bore into mine. It was now or never.

"Do you want more?" I asked.

His mouth curved into a dark smile. "Hell, yes."

"Good. But I need to talk to the bartender first."

2

WE STEPPED OUT of the pub, and I shivered in the cool evening air.

"Can we take the long way back to my hotel?" asked I. "I've never been to Stockholm before."

"Sure," he said. "Let's head up the hill."

We turned up a narrow cobblestone street. Jonas shoved his hands in his pockets and walked close by my side. I couldn't get over how big he was. It was impossible not to notice him. The guys we passed on the street stepped out of his way, and women sized him up. Jonas kept his head down, as if he didn't notice the attention. Or didn't care.

There were so many reasons why Jonas would make a terrible boyfriend. Starting with the way women looked at him. I'd spend too much time wondering if he'd look up one day and notice all the cute young things staring just a little too long. When the fun was over, he'd probably end up leaving me for someone softer. Younger.

But he wasn't my boyfriend. He was mine for now, for tonight. Anything after that didn't have to matter.

"I can't believe you asked the bartender for personal details about me," Jonas chuckled, his chest brushing against my shoulder as we passed a couple on the street.

I raised an eyebrow.

"At least he understood me this time," I said. "A woman can't be too careful these days. Besides, it's rather sweet to find out that you meet your mother there for dinner every Sunday."

Jonas barked out a laugh. "Sweet? That's a first."

"Not sweet?" I raised an eyebrow. "You're the writer. What word would you choose?"

He smiled a little, but he didn't answer. We headed down another side street that ended at a busy intersection. He stopped next to an old wooden doorway, and I turned back to look at him. His eyes were fiery and dark.

"You want to know what I'm like?" he asked.

I nodded and leaned against the building, waiting for whatever he was going to say. But he didn't say anything.

Jonas took a few steps closer, his eyes fixed on me. He moved slowly, giving me all the time in the world to back down. I didn't. He rested his hands against the wall on either side of me. His eyes grew heavy as he watched me. I drew in a shaky breath.

Damn, this was hot.

He moved closer and brought a hand to my face, the way he had in the pub. But this time he didn't stop. Slowly, gently, he caressed my cheek and traced the line of my lips with his thumb until I parted them. He tilted my chin up towards his. My gaze drifted up, over his long, thin scar, barely visible beneath a brush of stubble, up to his glittering blue eyes. They were fixed on mine again, hopeful but a little darker, as he lowered his wide, sensual mouth to mine. Warm. Inviting. I was dizzy with relief. Finally.

I opened my mouth and slid my tongue over his bottom lip. I slipped my fingers into his hair, and he groaned softly. His big hands moved over my hips, and I pressed myself flush to his long, hard body. His fingers tightened, and his kiss turned hungry. His tongue tasted mine, licking, promising more. The kiss in the pub didn't even come close to where we were going now. I tugged on his hair, holding on, as I took the kiss deeper.

A deep groan rumbled inside his chest. He pulled back and raked his teeth over my bottom lip.

"That's what I'm like," he whispered. "You want that?"

I nodded slowly, still dizzy from the kiss. "I think I'm done wandering through Stockholm. Let's go back to my hotel."

He smiled. "I'd better stop at the corner store first."

I WALKED SILENTLY down the fifth floor hall. Jonas said nothing. His large hand rested on my lower back, a physical reminder of what was coming.

I stopped in front of my room, and my fingers trembled as I searched my purse for my room key. Could I really go through with this? God, I wanted to. Just for tonight, I was back in high school, before my father had returned for the very last time. Before I had sworn off guys like Jonas. And it felt good.

Just one night. No danger of getting in too deep.

Besides, all of Jonas's charm could still be for his book, nothing more. The more we talked, the less likely this seemed. But even if this were true, Jonas's motives didn't matter. Tonight was my one chance to taste the other life I had turned away from.

When the lock finally clicked open, I looked up. Jonas's gaze was soft and steady.

"Are you ok?" he asked. "You can still call this off."

"I don't do things like this. Not even close," I said. "But I want to. I'm more nervous about what I want, not where I want to stop."

Jonas chuckled and traced the curve of my waist with his hand. "Sounds good to me."

We walked into the dark room, lit only by the lights from the city through the sheer curtains. I took a deep breath and turned to him, steadying my hands on his solid, broad chest. His heart pulsed beneath his shirt.

I smiled a little. "Maybe I should offer you the same. You can call this off, too."

Jonas shook his head slowly, and his eyes were heavy with lust.

"I'll do everything you can think of," he said his voice low. He brought his mouth down to brush the rim of my ear. "Everything."

Then he did it again—that kiss. The kiss from the street, with long, slow strokes of his tongue, each one erasing everything else except his body against mine.

I found his biceps and ran my thumbs up the hard bulges. Wow. It had been so long since I had touched someone like this, someone with such raw sex appeal. I was supposed to be long past this phase. And I was. But here in Stockholm, so far away from home, there was nothing wrong with a little indulgence. I wasn't a teenager anymore. I could handle it.

"You're so big," I whispered, stretching my hand over the planes of his muscles.

"You like that?" His breath teased my neck.

"Yeah."

His hands moved lower down my back. "Good."

He slid his hands under my rear and lifted me, his thick, muscular arms flexing hard under my fingers. *Whoa.* He was big everywhere. His erection, long and heavy, pressed against me, and I let out a little sigh of pleasure. His grip tightened, and I squirmed closer. He let out a deeper groan.

I closed my eyes and took one more breath of his scent. He released me, and I leaned against the wall, creating a little space between us. He reached out to brush a curl from my forehead and caressed my face.

"What do you like, Alice?"

What did I like? I had never really given the question any thought.

"What are my options?" I asked.

Jonas smiled darkly. "I just wanted to know if there was anything that really turns you on."

I shrugged. "The kind of things we're already doing, I guess."

Jonas nodded.

"What about you?" I asked. "What do you like?"

Jonas's eyes widened. "You know, I always ask women this question, and no one ever asks it back."

His gaze drifted lower as he shamelessly checked out my breasts. Was that his answer? He slipped his hand under the hem of my t-shirt and let his finger glide over my bare skin. A rush of heat ran through me.

"I like a lot of different things," he finally said. "I guess it depends on the person. How we are together. But I have this feeling that I'm really going to like you."

I stared up at him, searching for something to say. He was so direct. I had never once been with a guy who had come out and said he was into me. Guys like this didn't exist in New York, not in my old life and not in my new one.

He brushed his lips over mine. "Let's just see where this goes. But tell me if there's anything you don't like."

I nodded. He kissed me again and let his hand drop from my waist.

Jonas picked up the little bag he had dropped on the floor and carried it over to the nightstand. He sat down on the edge, not bothering to hide the erection throbbing between his thick, muscular thighs. If Jonas had looked out of place at the Stockholm Book Expo, he stood out just as much in this sleek, modern hotel room. But he didn't seem to care. He lifted his gaze and stared at me with unabashed interest. He tugged his t-shirt over his head, revealing muscles and tattoos and scars and a dark trail of hair that disappeared into his jeans.

I opened my mouth, but nothing came out. Jonas wore the traces of his past on his body, some chosen, others not. My heart pounded as I took a step forward. Where did he get his scars? In the pub, he had turned away another question about his past. He'd do the same if I came out and asked directly.

I took another step. "You're in really good shape. Especially for a writer."

He smiled a little. "Habit, I guess."

"Did you used to play sports?"

Jonas shook his head, and his smile faded. "Nothing like that. In the past, being big had a lot of advantages."

I swallowed and came closer. "In the past, but not now?"

"No, not now." He kept his gaze steady on me, intense and serious.

"Never again?" I whispered.

"Never again."

I nodded. What had he left behind? I had heard a lot of *never again* in my life, and it usually only lasted until the temptation was in sight again. But when Jonas said those words, I heard sadness, not temptation. The same *never again* that I had whispered to myself as I walked out of my mother's apartment for the last time. The loneliest kind of *never again*.

And Jonas knew this feeling, too. Something flickered in his eyes, something I recognized.

I froze, mid-step. What was I getting myself into?

But no matter what happened tonight, I was leaving the country tomorrow. Just one night wasn't enough to ruin everything I had turned away from, was it? I closed my eyes and steadied my breath.

I didn't know his story, and he didn't know mine. We were just two people, coming together for one night. One really good night, if I had any say in it.

I took a last step so I stood between his open legs. He was tall enough so that his face was level with my chest, even sitting down. I pulled off my own shirt, revealing a thin, lacy bra. My nipples poked through the fabric. Jonas parted his lips, and the heat of his breath traveled over my skin. But he didn't move. He waited. Despite the huge bulge in his pants, he didn't seem to be in any hurry.

"Can I—" I started. "Can I sit on your lap?"

"Please." His voice came out a little hoarse.

Jonas shifted further back onto the bed. I climbed on top of him until I straddled him. I rested my hands on the thick muscles of his shoulders. His hands caressed my hips, the muscles of his chest flexing under his movements.

"You're gorgeous," I whispered.

His eyes widened. He was silent as creases formed on his brow. "Not usually the kind of response I get."

I nodded. A long scar cut through a tribal-like tattoo by his shoulder, through the dusting of hair across his chest. I drifted my fingers down to trace it. His pulse pounded at the base of his throat, but he didn't move.

"How do people usually describe you?" When I asked a version of this last time, he kissed me. This time?

The creases on his forehead deepened. "Intense. Probably a lot of other shit I don't want to hear. Nothing like gorgeous."

"But you are," I said.

He shrugged like he didn't quite believe me. "Okay."

I traced the inked lines of a Celtic cross, woven together with bright drops of blood. Above it, a thick black bird flew away into untouched skin. He flinched a little when I touched the bird, so I explored further down. Phrases. Intricate designs. In faded black script, I found the word *Norr*.

"What does this mean?" I asked, following the slopes and arches of each letter with my fingers.

Jonas smiled. "That was my first tattoo. It means North, the area of town where I grew up."

"Sounds like a gang."

He laughed. "We wished we were."

He covered my hand with his as I moved over his skin. "*Norr* is a sprawl of run-down apartments, and we all had a rougher reputation, though not for any good reason. Then a couple of us got into the top high school, including me." He gave me a sideways glance. Did he think I wouldn't believe he was a good student? His writing skills had to come from somewhere.

He moved my hand a little lower. "We all got this tattoo after we realized we'd get the shit beaten out of us if we all didn't look a little tougher. Both at school and back at *Norr*."

I raised an eyebrow as I followed the hard ridges of his abs. "Looks like your plan worked."

He shrugged. "I took a lot of bad hits before I started figuring it all out."

Jonas caressed my cheek. He slid his fingers down my throat and along my collar bone. He traced the edge of my bra, over one breast and then the other.

"You look pretty amazing, too," he said. "But all the other words that come to mind are going to sound crass."

I smiled. "I don't mind."

"I do." He cupped my breast and teased my nipple with his thumb. I sucked in a breath, and he groaned.

"Can I take off your bra?" he asked.

I nodded. He leaned forward, and his chest brushed against my bare skin as he unlatched my bra.

My breasts tumbled out, and Jonas drew in an uneven breath as he moved the straps down my arms. He traced the slope of each breast with his fingers, sending currents of pleasure through my body. He pulled me up higher against him and kissed a path down my shoulder and over my breast. I arched, moving, pressing myself into him, until finally he took my nipple in his mouth. His tongue caressed me slowly, sucking until I moaned.

He released me and buried his face in my neck. I pressed against his fever-hot skin, his heartbeat pounding as hard as mine. His voice was tight when he spoke, and there was nothing polished about his accent now.

"I want to do this right with you, Alice. I don't want to get carried away."

"I wouldn't mind," I said.

His rough fingers trembled as he ran his hands down my arms, pulling me closer.

"I want you to enjoy this so much that you can't stop yourself from coming back for more."

I froze. I drew in a quick breath and pulled away. I wasn't coming back to Stockholm.

"But that's not how this works," I said slowly.

He frowned and looked away. "Sorry. That just came out."

I reached up to stroke his cheek.

"It's okay," I said. "This feels really good. But it isn't the real version of either of us, right?"

My heart thumped harder as I waited for his response. It took a moment, but his frown softened, and he nodded.

He slid his hands over my shoulders and reached to cup my chin. He tilted my mouth up for a long, liquid kiss that dissolved his comment. He kissed my jawbone and my neck. If he was waiting to gauge my hesitation, he wasn't going to find any. I left that back at the pub.

I slipped my hand between us, playing with the trail of hair that ran down into his pants. I dipped my fingers lower, slowly running my hand over the rough material of his jeans and down the length of him. His mouth brushed against mine. His lips found my neck, and he sucked and bit as his hand glided over my breast.

"This is up to you, Alice," he whispered in my ear. "You know I want you badly. Do you want to take this further?"

I nodded.

It didn't take more than that. He rolled me over in one quick motion so I lay on my back with Jonas hovering over me on all fours. His deep blue eyes steady, he lowered his body until his hot skin brushed against mine. I arched my back again, craving the contact. His mouth took mine in long, hungry strokes. He sucked and nipped at my lips, and my whole body responded.

I reached down and fumbled with the button of my jeans, but he caught both of my hands in one of his.

"Slowly, Alice," he said.

He shifted down my body, his tongue tracing a line over each breast, around my navel, to the edge of my jeans. My breaths came faster, louder. He unbuttoned them and drew down the zipper. He took a deep breath and let it out, the warm air tingling lower through the lace of my panties. I shivered.

He was taking his time. Way too much time.

"Jonas?" My voice cracked.

He stopped and looked up at me, his eyes dark. "Do you know what you want yet, *Alice*?"

Answers came to my mind, places I wanted to explore, positions I had heard hints about. I wanted the part of me who said yes to this whole crazy evening. And right now was my chance. I could say whatever I wanted, and it wouldn't matter.

"I want you to taste me," I whispered. "And I want to know what you taste like. I want to know how turned on I get if I take you in my mouth and suck hard."

Jonas's eyes widened, and my face burned.

"*Fuck*," he growled and mumbled a few other words I didn't understand.

I pushed myself to continue. "But what I want most is to be the woman who asks for all these things."

His tongue brushed against the top of my panties, and my hips responded, searching for more. But he didn't give it to me.

"Do you know what I want?" Jonas rumbled. "I want to be the man who makes these fantasies real for you. And I want to do things you've never even thought of."

I lifted my hips, and he eased my jeans down my legs. They didn't exactly slide off. Note to self: don't wear tight jeans if you're bringing a man back to your hotel room. Not that a night like this would ever happen again.

I scooted further onto the bed, and Jonas knelt between my legs. He unzipped his pants and reached inside to adjust himself. His long, thick erection poked out of the top of his boxers. I bit my lip. This promised to be… fulfilling.

He leaned forward onto his elbows, and I widened my legs to accommodate his broad shoulders. He stared at my lacy panties, his hot breath teasing me. I grabbed the sheets. Slowly, he moved the tiny scrap of fabric aside until I was bare. With his other hand, he traced me up and down. I squirmed and dug in my feet when he reached the top, so he stayed there, exploring. I was so wound up I wasn't sure what would happen when he actually started.

He leaned in. His tongue passed over every sensitive inch of me. I pulled the sheets and moaned loudly. He sucked and licked slowly, luxuriously. I twisted under his movements until one firm hand held me down. Sparks of electricity shot through me as I wriggled but went nowhere.

Oh, God.

I wriggled again, and he held me down harder. Something flipped inside, and all at once, my body ignited. The burst of pleasure came all at once. Sudden. Intense. I let out a loud cry, somewhere between ecstasy and surprise, and my head fell back onto the bed. I moaned and twisted as he drew me out. I clawed at the sheets and whispered his name.

Seconds or minutes passed as the warm bliss flooded through me. Wow. The whole night had been a long, slow build, but the moment he held me down...

Jonas sat back on his knees and gave his erection a long stroke.

"That was hot," he murmured. "Really hot."

"I didn't expect...," I panted, searching for words. "It's been a while for me."

I propped myself up on my elbows to get a good look at Jonas. His muscles were tight and flexed, and his erection was stiff under his hand, but he didn't move closer. How could I still want more? But instead of settling me, the intense burst just minutes before got me going. Was this what I had missed out on all these years? I had wanted the other side of myself tonight, and I couldn't deny that I found it.

My voice was still breathless when I spoke. "Are we taking this further, or do I need to beg for more?"

Jonas's low, sensual laugh rumbled. "I like the idea of begging, Alice. We can play with it later. But right now, I want you too bad to wait for it."

He crawled off the bed and shed his jeans and boxers in one move. Whoa. I hadn't just imagined it. Like everything else on him, his erection was huge. I stared, far beyond embarrassment. He climbed back between my legs and settled his body over mine, brushing against me in all the right places.

Despite the urgency of his words, he still took his time. He teased my mouth with long, sensuous thrusts of his tongue, nipping and sucking at my lips. I arched my hips to meet his thick erection, and he groaned as he ground over my aching core. I ran my fingers over the scarred, tattooed muscles of his chest. Did he like things rough? The firm hand on my hips as he held me down suggested he might. But despite the tightly wound power under my hands, he seemed to be looking for something else than rough from me tonight. What was it?

"You bought a condom when we stopped at that store, right?" I asked.

He nodded. "More than one."

"How many?" I whispered.

He smiled. "Ten in a box."

"Hmm... ten. That's ambitious."

His erection was rock hard now and pulsing against me as I spoke.

"I'll do my best," he said with a little laugh.

He met my lips once more and then reached for the bag on the nightstand. Tearing the wrapping from the condom, he rolled it down his length and then held himself for a moment, watching me.

"Is this what you like?" he said with a wicked hint of a smile. He settled back against me, guiding himself to me.

"Yes," I gulped.

Then he pushed, sinking in. He hissed a sigh and squeezed his eyes shut as he pushed further.

"Oh," I breathed. The hot, sweet relief. The heavy weight of his body. I had been waiting for this moment all night, and I didn't even know it. He was so big and thick inside me. There was still more, and I grabbed onto the hard muscles of his arms and squeezed tighter. His eyes were wild and hungry.

"You okay?" he groaned.

"Yes."

"I want this to be good for you," he said. "I want it to be better than good."

"It already is."

He began to move, slowly teasing. I lifted my hips to match his strokes. He gritted his teeth and thrust hard. Oh, God, again? I moaned and he thrust harder. I cried out, and he froze, his eyes filled with fear.

I shook my head quickly and caressed his face.

"Better than good, Jonas," I panted. "Don't stop."

He nodded, but the wariness in his eyes didn't go away. He started to move again, building a rhythm, but his wild look was gone. The tight muscles of his arms flexed, and his pulse pounded in the base of his neck.

He lowered himself to his elbows, changing the angle, and flexed his hips against mine. He took one of my breasts in his mouth and sucked. I arched, begging for more.

"I've been hard for you all day long," he groaned. "I just knew this would feel right."

He squeezed my breasts and pinched my nipples each time he thrust. Better than good. It was the way he looked at me, as if I were the only woman he'd ever want. That he'd give me everything I needed.

He shifted, slipping his arms under me, his hands around my shoulders. I tilted my hips to meet each of his movements, to find a way closer. His heavy breaths mixed with mine, and he buried his face in my neck. I closed my eyes and lost myself in the scent of sex and him. Hard cords of muscles contracted under my hands as his body moved faster. Deeper.

I was close, so close.

"Oh," I breathed. "*Jonas*."

At the sound of his name, his big body tightened. In one giant growl, he erupted, driving, pushing me over the edge. His teeth sank into my neck, and I cried out. I clung to him as he drove in heavy thrusts, drawing out my pleasure.

3

I LAY ON my back. My hair sprang out in all different directions over the pillow, but for once, I didn't care. Jonas lay on his side, his slick body up against mine, playing with a stray curl. His other hand rested on my hip, his thumb gently stroking my skin.

I looked up into his dark blue eyes. "We should probably get some sleep."

"Not on my account." He chuckled. "Did I tell you I love your sexy hair?"

I rolled my eyes. "It drives me crazy."

"Good," he said. "Me, too."

He took a fistful in his hands and pulled my mouth to his for a hard kiss. Biting my bottom lip, he slowly let me go.

He propped himself on one elbow and rubbed his forehead, flexing his long, thick bicep. My fingers wandered over the thick black bird on his chest again. This time he didn't flinch. I hadn't noticed earlier that one of its wings was broken. It was an odd choice for something as permanent as a tattoo.

I opened my mouth to ask more, but I closed it, frowning. There was no reason to learn more about his tattoos or anything else. In a few hours, I would leave for the airport, and the details about his life wouldn't matter anymore. In fact, it was probably better not to know. Instead, I closed my eyes and breathed in his warm scent.

"I knew it would feel right, too," I said after a while.

Jonas stilled, and I opened my eyes to get a look at his expression.

I added, "You said it earlier, when—"

"I remember what I said." His hand dropped.

"Sorry," I said and looked away. "That was too much."

He coaxed my face back in his direction with his big, warm hand. "Not too much at all."

I studied him. His eyes were soft but guarded.

Finally he shook his head. "This does feel right. Really right. I'm just thinking about all the ways it could go."

I snorted. "Are you talking positions?"

Jonas raised his eyebrows and smiled a little. "I wasn't, but I'm up for that discussion as well. I'm talking about what happens tomorrow."

"Tomorrow I'm leaving," I said flatly.

"It doesn't have to be like that."

But it *was* like that. I was leaving for Copenhagen, and the next day I'd fly back to New York. The end. No matter how good or right this felt.

"Look, I have a long history of getting tangled up with things that feel good," he said. "The results are mixed. So I'm a little wary of what I'm about to say."

I raised an eyebrow, waiting silently. Jonas bent down and let his lips brush against mine. "Are you sure you want me to continue? We only have a few more hours together."

It would be easier not to talk about what ifs and maybes. Back in New York, I would have said no. In fact, I would have left Jonas behind in the pub. I knew the kinds of mistakes a woman could make with a man like Jonas. My mother had made them. My best friend had made them. On every corner of my old neighborhood I could find new ways to screw up the future in exchange for something that felt good. And I had sworn off that temptation. But that had never stopped me from wondering if those moments were worth it.

I studied Jonas's eyes. They were soft and a little sad. He had his own answers to my questions.

"I want to hear it," I said.

"Okay." Jonas nodded. He rubbed his jaw along the faded scar line. "I have this hunger inside, a part of me that can't get enough. And I'm not always sure what will get it going. It took a long time for me to even understand this. I was into all sorts of trouble when I was younger."

I smiled a little. "And now you're older and wiser, and you stay away from those things?"

Jonas chuckled. "Sometimes it's the kind of shit that everyone knows is trouble, and these days I'm not stupid enough to think I can handle it. I know I can't." He rested his hand on my hip and stroked my skin slowly with his thumb. "But every now and then I get hooked on something that's good for me. Like writing books. When I started, I had a lot of time and not a lot of options. The stories were all I thought about for a long, long time. I wrote nine books that first year."

"Impressive," I said. "Most authors would be happy with one good book a year."

He shrugged. The muted honks of a car horn came from the street below.

"Why are you bringing this up?" I asked softly.

A crease formed on his brow. He stroked my hair and pressed his lips against mine, opening for a slow caress with his tongue. He pulled back and smiled a little. "Feel free to kick me out if this gets too intense."

I smiled. "I'll keep that in mind."

Jonas took a deep breath. "I feel it happening now. With you. Even though we just met. Like this night isn't enough. And I don't know whether to keep my mouth shut and walk out right now or beg you to stay another day."

His words hummed inside me. I wanted it. I wanted to be reckless. Just to see what it felt like.

He took his hand out of my hair and watched me wearily. He bowed his head. "That was too much, wasn't it?"

I swallowed. "Even if we wanted to play this out for one more day, I'm leaving for Copenhagen tomorrow. And I fly back to New York on Saturday morning."

He nodded, still not meeting my eyes.

I cupped his cheeks in my hands, and he looked up at me again with his dark blue eyes. What would happen if I found a way to see Jonas again? I wouldn't end up crazy and desperate like my best friend. I wouldn't end up pregnant and alone like my mother.

I stroked Jonas's cheek and traced his strong jaw line. It wouldn't change anything back in New York. I could take this chance, just to see what it would be like.

"Maybe I could change my ticket home," I said quietly. "Maybe we could find a way to meet up before I go back."

His eyes were fixed on mine, but he didn't say anything. He didn't move. The only sign of emotion was his pulse, pounding hard at the base of his neck.

"And you want to try that?" he said in a hoarse whisper.

I swallowed harder. "Yes."

Jonas nodded slowly. "Okay." His eyes softened, and he held my gaze. "What about Paris?"

I blinked. "Really?"

The city of lights? My dream destination? It was impulsive, exactly the kind of thing I'd never do.

He cleared his throat. "Yes, Paris. If we're doing this, let's do it all the way."

"Paris," I echoed. "Um, okay. Yes."

Jonas's face opened into a smile. "Are you sure?"

I wrinkled my brow. "I'm not sure about anything right now."

He sat up in bed and ruffled his hand through his hair. He squeezed my leg.

"I'll figure out the details," he said. "Just get yourself to Paris the day after tomorrow. I'll meet you in the airport and we'll go from there."

I sat up and brushed my hair off my shoulders. We were going to Paris. Just like that.

"Wow," I said softly. "Just...wow."

Jonas ran his hand up and down my thigh. I watched his thick, tribal-like tattoo curve and bend as his bicep muscles flexed. I traced the thick lines around his arm.

He glanced down where my fingers met his skin, and his smile faded. "Listen, you asked me about my past. You can look it up while you're in Copenhagen, or we can talk about it when we get to Paris. It's up to you."

I blinked. I was more than a little curious about this man. But if I started to dig, what would I find?

Jonas's gaze never left me. "If you read something that makes you change your mind about being in the same room as me, I'll understand."

If I had any doubts about what his past looked like, they were gone. I knew a hundred versions of this story, and they were all bad. Did it matter? I had already taken this man up to my hotel room. Just one more night, and it would be over.

"One more night," I said.

He nodded slowly.

I laced my hand in his and climbed on top of him, settling against the hard wall of his chest. He buried his face in my hair and breathed out a long sigh. His other hand traveled up and down my side, pulling my closer. His erection was growing again, pressing against me in all the right places. He circled his thumb over my nipple in long, slow strokes. I let out a quiet moan. His lips found the tender slope of my neck.

"Even if this isn't who we are, it's real," he whispered. "More real than anything I've felt in a long time."

Jonas's words echoed through me, lingering long after I had left the hotel room, triggering dangerous aftershocks of hope and want.

SEDUCTION

1

I SCANNED THE arrivals hall of Charles De Gaulle Airport for the hundredth time. The monitor told me that his plane arrived forty-five minutes ago. Or, rather, the plane he was supposed to take. Because clearly he hadn't gotten on it. The baggage carousel was empty. All the other passengers had left.

No message. He just hadn't shown up.

I dialed his number for the third time. For the third time, the call went straight to voicemail. I didn't leave a third message. No more telling myself he just hadn't turned on his phone yet. There was no way around it. He had stood me up.

I looked around the empty carousel once more. Everyone from the Stockholm flight was long gone. How stupid could I be? Up all night, wondering how to ask Jonas for the things I wanted to try. Things I'd always been curious about. Never once considering he might not come.

I sat down on my suitcase and closed my eyes. Of course Jonas was too good to be true. How many guys did I know exactly like him? Just because he said something in bed didn't mean he'd actually follow through. Even if that something involved a trip to a foreign country.

Now I was in Paris, the destination of my dreams, and that wasn't enough. I wanted Jonas, too.

I gritted my teeth and stood up. Just get over it and move on. So what if it was Jonas who was supposed to arrange the hotel room? So what if I couldn't speak a word of French? I could walk out to the curb and say the words *Eiffel Tower* to the taxi driver. And forget about all the things I wanted to do with Jonas.

I took a deep breath, straightened up and grabbed the handle of my suitcase. Why was I surprised? This was nothing new. How many times did my mother fall apart when my father didn't show up? And how many times did I blame my mother, who should have known better? Now I waited alone in the arrivals hall, stood up by my own ex-con. But I wasn't going to fall apart, not here. I yanked my suitcase toward the doorway.

"*Alice?*" A voice echoed across the hall.

I drew in a shaky breath. *Don't get your hopes up.* I turned around and braced myself.

Jonas. He pushed his way through the crowd on the escalator and jogged across the arrivals hall. His hair was sticking out in all directions, as if he had run his hand through it too many times. The thick muscles of his arm flexed under the weight of his duffle bag, and his intense blue eyes shone. He was here. He hadn't stood me up.

My heart flipped and fluttered and raced with relief, damn it.

He came in fast and crushed me in a clumsy embrace. "You're still here."

"Just barely."

He held me against his chest until I softened into him. I should be mad, but the frustration was slipping away, and in its place, my body awakened. I was way too into this guy.

Jonas pulled me closer. "I'm sorry. I got on an earlier flight. It was supposed to be a surprise, but then the flight got diverted, and… shit, so much went wrong." He released me and mumbled something incomprehensible. "But you're still here."

I nodded, trying to wipe the relief off my face. Of course he had an excuse, a good one. Enough to keep me hoping. That was how this worked.

He kissed me softly. "I hope that means I haven't messed this up too badly."

I closed my eyes and shook my head.

"Not yet, at least." He sighed. "Let's get out of here."

THE TAXI TURNED from a maze of backstreets into a large cobblestone courtyard with trees and old-fashioned street lamps. Restaurants spilled out into the square on every side, some empty, some with a few lingering guests.

Jonas said something incomprehensible to the driver. That was three languages and counting for him. Not what I expected from a man marked with tattoos and scars. But nothing about Jonas was what I expected.

Cool off, Alice. This was the guy who almost stood me up. Even if he hadn't meant to, I had a taste of just how much I wanted a day together in Paris. And how quickly I'd forgive him at the promise of one more night. Every time that deep, sexy mix of Swedish and Irish accents came out of his mouth, all reason disappeared.

How many times did I consider backing out yesterday? Umm, zero. My first taste of him blew every other experience out of the water. Give up an opportunity to see where one more night would take us? Not a chance.

We pulled up in front of an old stone building at the far corner of the plaza. I slipped out of the cab onto the sidewalk, and Jonas followed. The driver, an older man in a vest and a white collared shirt, carried my suitcase and Jonas's small duffle bag to the curb.

"Thank you," I said.

The old man ignored me and headed back to his open door.

Jonas's deep laugh rumbled. "Welcome to Paris."

"And its well-known friendliness?"

"Exactly."

He held my gaze, and his smile turned into something else. His hands slid down my neck to my shoulders. I reached up and traced the thin scar along his jaw. Maybe I'd find a way to ask about that. And more.

I rose on my toes and pulled myself closer to his full lips. Jonas let out a deep sigh. He leaned down and pressed his mouth softly against mine, lingering for an extra breath. Just being this close was intoxicating. I slipped my other hand under the hem of his shirt, grabbing onto the warm, hard muscles beneath.

He slid his hands down my arms and over my hips. He bent down again and parted his mouth, and I tasted his warm, sweet breath. His tongue moved in soft strokes over mine, and I moaned. The strokes grew longer, deeper until he bit down on my lip, hard enough to startle me. I gasped as a ripple of pleasure traveled through me.

He froze and let me go. "Sorry."

"No. Don't be," I whispered.

Jonas studied me for a moment, his gaze heating up. His muscles tightened and twitched under my hand. Darker want, simmering need shone in his eye. And then it was gone. He straightened up and looked away. He picked up his duffle bag and rubbed the back of his neck. I tucked a wisp of stray curls behind my ear and grabbed the handle of my suitcase. Neither of us spoke. I met his gaze again. The hard lines of his jaw had softened, but his dark blue eyes were guarded now.

I searched for something to say. "So, here we are in Paris."

Jonas's eyes stayed on mine for an extra beat. Then the corners of his mouth turned up. "What do you want to do first?"

"I'm aching for a nap, but it feels like a waste of Paris," I said.

"Start the day in bed?" Jonas's smile grew. "Definitely not a waste of Paris."

Good point. I had stayed awake too late in Copenhagen, wondering what one more night with him would be like. If I got a quick nap, I could make it all night again. I had the rest of my life in New York to sleep. Though probably none of the things running through his head right had to do with sleep.

Jonas pulled open the glass door, and we walked into the hotel's little lobby. Not at all ostentatious. Which hopefully translated to affordable.

"Give me a minute," he said. "I just want to work something out with the receptionist."

Jonas headed for the pixie-like woman behind the front desk. The low cadence of his voice traveled through the cramped lobby. I couldn't understand a word of what he said, but I didn't miss the woman's look as Jonas leaned over the counter.

Even on a good day, I couldn't fake the effortless style of this cute little bombshell with a sleek black bob. And today? I was so far from effortless style I was surprised the French fashion police let me off the airplane. I reached for the halo of frizz that had escaped from my bun.

I pulled out the hair fastener to corral the stray curls. But wait. I had the rest of my life to be *that* Alice. The Alice that blew her hair straight every morning and kept it pinned back so she looked more serious. One more day to be a different version of myself. I took out my bun and shook my hair free. It was still damp from the shower, and I combed through it a few times with my fingers, coaxing flyaway curls back in line.

Jonas's deep voice came again. The receptionist's eyes darted to Jonas's bare muscular forearms, then back up to his eyes. I couldn't blame her. But what did Jonas think about the look on the woman's face? This wasn't the first woman I had caught checking him out. Maybe he noticed the lingering glances, the flush creeping up the woman's neck, but he wasn't reacting.

If Jonas were my boyfriend, it would drive me crazy to watch the way women ogled him. But he wasn't my boyfriend. Not even close.

Jonas and the woman were silent now, but the conversation clearly wasn't over. The receptionist blinked her doe-like eyes and bit her lip. I sighed. Her voice was soft and musical. Of course it was. She was conceding something. Then she reached behind her, grabbed a key, and placed it in Jonas's hand.

"*Merci.*"

Jonas turned around. His eyes met mine, and his face opened up into a smile. My heart thumped in my chest.

"Ready?" He grabbed both our bags and signaled toward the hallway.

I nodded and followed after him.

The tiny elevator was either charming or run-down, depending on the perspective. I wasn't sure where I stood on the matter. Out of the corner of my eye, I caught Jonas watching me.

"I love your hair like this," he said. He wove his hand into my curls. "Even more than when it was straight at the Expo."

I smiled. "Thanks. And I love to see you turn on your charm. You had that receptionist's attention."

"Mmm," he said kissing me again. "But I'm not so good with women."

I raised an eyebrow. "You've got to be kidding." I brushed my hand over the muscles across his chest. "You're the definition of eye candy."

Jonas chuckled. "I mean beyond that. I can be a little intense, if you hadn't noticed." He gave me a wry smile.

Yes, he was intense. So far, I had only seen the upsides. But I had caught a couple glimpses of that hard, cold look on his face in Stockholm. He had that side, too, but if I knew anything about a man like Jonas, the bad parts would come later. And there was no later. How many times was I going to remind myself of that?

The elevator jolted to a stop, and I stepped out. Jonas gestured down the hallway. Toward the bedroom.

Where I was going to ask for the things I'd never ask for in real life.

"In Stockholm everyone spoke English," I said, stalling. "Why do I get the feeling that isn't going to work here?"

Jonas shrugged. "People are a lot friendlier if you attempt a little French."

"I took Spanish in college," I said. "Much more useful in New York."

Jonas set down his bag in front of a doorway and crossed his arms. "Let's do something about that. Ready for your crash course in French?"

"Now? Here?" I asked, glancing down the hallway.

"Just three phrases."

Well, that didn't sound impossible. I put my hands on my hips. "I'm ready."

Jonas's gaze drifted down my body and snapped back up. He smiled. "Right. Number one: If you bump into someone, say *pardon*."

"*Pardon*," I repeated. "Got it."

"Good." Jonas's smile grew. "Number two: If you need someone's attention, say *excusez-moi*."

"*Excusez-moi*. Okay," I said. "But if I get anyone's attention, I'm at the end of my French. So I doubt I'll use that."

Jonas shook his head. "That's where number three comes in. If you want something, you just say please—*s'il vous plait*—and then point at whatever you need."

I snorted. "That's all the French I need?"

"Mmm. You can have extra credit lessons on bedroom talk later." He gave my ass a squeeze.

I rolled my eyes, but my cheeks flushed. Bedroom talk. Something to look forward to in any language.

"Are you ready for our Paris room?" He moved closer, his mouth almost touching mine. He licked his lips and leaned in for a soft, almost chaste kiss. His hand glided up my arm, leaving a trail of heat. He kissed me again, long and slow. *This* was right. This feeling, right now, was the reason I had changed my travel plans.

I tangled my fingers in his soft, thick hair and pulled him closer. I pressed against his big, solid body, but it wasn't enough. His tongue found mine for a few, luscious strokes before he broke off the kiss. He leaned his forehead against mine.

"We should probably make it into the room before we start with that," he said, his voice husky and low. "My plan was to resist this kind of temptation until you had a chance to see the view. But I'm losing my resolve."

He ran his hand over my frizzy hair.

"Beautiful," he said and brought a springy lock to his lips. He let me go and opened the door.

2

THE ROOM WAS charming, just short of shabby, with enough old sconces and flourishes on the walls to compensate for its size. The wrought-iron bed took up most of the space, with barely enough room to walk around its sides. Jonas set our bags down and tested the bounce of the mattress with his hands.

He smiled and raised an eyebrow. "Hope this holds up tonight."

I rolled my eyes.

"And now for the best part," he said, holding out his hand for me to join him at the French doors in the corner of the room. He opened the doors, and we stepped out into the warm, humid breeze together.

"Wow," I whispered. I couldn't have dreamed up a better view if I tried. Old, elegant buildings rose up all around us, but our particular balcony faced a lower rooftop, which opened up the line of sight directly to the Seine and the Eiffel Tower.

"Quite a view, right?" said Jonas, squeezing my hand. "I promised you it would be amazing and affordable. I hope it meets all other expectations as well."

"I'm sure it will," I said softly.

I looked over at the next balcony down from ours. They could probably see the Eiffel Tower as well, but the view wouldn't be nearly as good. This was all too good to be true—the perfect view from our balcony, the feel of his body so close to mine, and Jonas himself.

"This must be the best room in the hotel," I whispered.

"That's what I was negotiating with that receptionist."

"How did you—" An unwanted thought broke through the magic. "Have you been here before?"

Jonas's eyes widened for a moment, and then his brow furrowed. "Yes."

"With another woman?"

His whole body tensed. "Yes."

"Is it in your book?"

"Yes." Something flashed across his face. Anger? Frustration? It disappeared before I fully registered it.

I closed my eyes. I knew better than to hope for our own private romance from a guy like this, yet somehow I still had. But he had done this with other women, blindsided them with his Viking warrior body and his intense stare. He even had a special room for Paris trysts. Which anyone could read about in his book.

I turned and looked straight into Jonas's stormy blue eyes. Too many questions were reeling through my mind. I blurted one out. "Are you married?"

Both of his eyebrows shot up. "Married? No, not at all." He ran his hand through his hair, and his eyes searched mine. "You think I'd be here with you if I were married?"

"I guess not," I said quietly. "I just thought this was..."

Jonas nodded slowly. He walked back into the room and sat on the bed, gesturing for me to follow. I couldn't unsay the question, and now we were stuck in a hotel room together with it. But the last thing I wanted to talk about was his past exploits.

I forced my expression to business neutral and sat down, not letting myself touch him. I smoothed the white bedspread with my hand.

He rested his forearms on his knees and looked over at me. "Ask whatever you want." His voice was colder, detached. Wary.

"So you're not married. But you've brought another woman to this room to have sex on this bed. And you wrote about it."

He rubbed the deep lines in his forehead. "If we're going to get that specific, then no, I haven't had sex on this bed. Or in the bathroom or on the balcony, for that matter."

I narrowed my eyes. "So what type of a relationship did you have with this woman, who came to a beautiful, romantic hotel with you but didn't have sex?"

"She was my girlfriend, but the relationship was over." Jonas frowned. "We had our last fight at a restaurant down the street from here. After dinner, she came back to the room to get her bag and left. So I spent the night alone."

His voice was a whisper when he spoke this last word. Alone. It echoed through the hotel room, through my frustration, and it told me more than anything else he had said since Stockholm. For a moment, he looked defeated. Vulnerable.

"So you spent the night getting over your ex-girlfriend?" I asked softly. "Why would you bring me here?"

Jonas shook his head.

"That's not how I spent the night," he said softly. "I was pretty depressed. I kept fucking up my life, but I didn't care enough to change that. So I fucked it up worse."

He hung his head and rubbed the back of his neck. The muscles of his arms flexed as he moved and shifted.

Jonas turned his head to look at me, his eyes soft and serious. "I've always wanted to do things differently, to come back to Paris and make it right. And I want to be here with someone…"

His voice trailed off, leaving only the hard thumping of my heart in my ears. I kept my eyes steady on his. "With someone...?"

The creases on his forehead deepened. "I want to be here with you. I want us to explore whatever this is between us. I've messed up so much in my life. I want to get something right."

I smoothed more imaginary wrinkles out of the bedspread. I had promised myself not to look into Jonas's past.

Jonas rested his hand on mine, stopping my fidgeting. I swallowed. I turned my hand over and laced my fingers with his.

"I didn't look you up when I was in Copenhagen," I said. "I didn't think it was any of my business."

Jonas ran his other hand through his hair and took a long breath, his heavy shoulders rising and falling. "But it is."

"Even if you and I go our separate ways tomorrow?" I asked. "It doesn't matter."

"I said back in Stockholm that I wasn't the man in the story anymore, and it's mostly true. I won't let it happen again." He frowned. "But I'll never be able to get away from my past. Not even for one night, it turns out."

My fingers curled around the bedspread. "What should I know about you?"

"I spent some time in prison," he said flatly.

My heart gave a heavy thump. I had been right. I couldn't escape that world. Across the Atlantic, in a different country, with a different language, I had managed to find the kind of guy I'd sworn I'd never be with.

I swallowed hard. "What were you in for?"

He closed his eyes. "Drugs. Assault. I got into some trouble for some bad, stupid shit before, but this time was worse."

"How long ago?"

"I got out a couple years ago," he said, his shoulders sinking. He opened his eyes again and studied me. "You don't look as shocked as I thought you would. Though I haven't gotten into the details."

I hadn't taken a breath in too long. My heart pounded hard, but I wasn't shocked. Not even surprised, as if some part of me knew it from the start.

"And you're not into that stuff anymore?"

"No."

Of course not. That's what everyone said. That's what my father told my mother until the next time he got caught.

"Never again?" I asked.

He shook his head. "I managed to make it out the other side clean. I don't think I'll get a second chance on that kind of thing. It's been a long time, but I have to be careful."

There was wariness in his voice. As if he still didn't trust himself.

Jonas took a deep breath. "I'm really careful with what I get myself involved in. I throw myself into everything I do. I can be a little obsessive when something really clicks with me."

I almost smiled. He certainly hadn't hidden that part of himself.

"But as I told you back in Stockholm, sometimes the thing I get hooked on is something good." He smiled a little. "That's what I'm doing here in this hotel room."

My heart was beating so fast in my chest.

"The thing that really clicks with me right now is you." His expression softened. "But I understand if this changes things for us."

He was giving me an escape route. I could end it, walk away right now. I probably should.

He looked down at his hands. "It's fine. I get it. When I think about my past, I don't want to be around me either."

I closed my eyes. Why wasn't I getting up? My whole childhood had been a slow, painful lesson in where a relationship with a man like this went. But I wasn't my mother, and this wasn't a relationship. It was one more night.

I looked up into his eyes. "You didn't tell me about your past back in Stockholm because you thought I'd run?"

"Maybe. I had other selfish reasons, too." He parted his full lips, and for a moment I thought he might kiss me. Instead, he frowned. "I just wanted to see what it was like to be together, you and me, without my past, my mistakes. I have the rest of my life for remorse."

"What did that feel like?" I asked softly. "To forget for the night?"

"Good. Really good."

I took a deep breath and scooted closer on the bed. His arms closed around me, and I rested my head against his chest.

"But when I saw you at the airport today, I regretted it," he said, his breath in my hair. "Your whole face lit up when you smiled at me. But it was just for the cleaned-up version of me. Not everything."

A car revved its engine somewhere far below on the street. Jonas's chest rose and fell in slow, resigned breaths. The warmth of his arms felt so good. I could spend the whole day just like this.

Jonas shifted back a little. "Does this mean you're going to stay?"

I should have hesitated, but I didn't. "Yes."

"Good," he said, kissing the top of my head. "Good."

There were so many pieces of him that I would never know. In Stockholm, I told myself that Jonas was the kind of indulgence I could handle every once in a while without consequences, like chocolate or bad TV. But now I was sitting in a Paris hotel room, listening to his heart beat in his chest. This wasn't indulgence. This was something else.

"What are we doing, Jonas?" I whispered.

He smoothed my hair a couple times. "I don't know."

He eased back onto the bed, and I climbed around to settle next to him. I slipped my hand under his shirt and rested it on his hot skin. I closed my eyes and listened to the sound of his long, steady breaths.

3

I BLINKED A couple times, and everything came into focus. The afternoon sun lit a trail from the open French doors, onto the white bedspread, up Jonas's delicious body. His breaths were slow and steady in my ear. I was really here in a Paris hotel room, lying in Jonas's arms. Not a dream.

The taut planes of muscles under my fingers weren't a dream, either. My breath quickened.

I shifted to roll off the bed, trying not to wake him. I stretched and stepped into the sun. The balcony was warm, and the light skimmed and glittered over the rooftops. The Eiffel Tower, the real thing, rose up in the distance, shining.

I turned to take in Jonas's long, muscular frame, stretched out over the bed as he slept. There were no traces of the worry lines I had seen when we had talked about his past, and his full lips parted slightly in the same way they did when he was going to kiss me. One arm was thrown over his head, the lines of his thick muscles at rest, and his other arm lay out in silent invitation. I moved closer, studying the tattoos that wound around his arm. The thick tribal designs were the most prominent, and the ink was older, faded. What did he think of these tattoos now that he had left his old life behind?

His shirt had risen up, exposing the lean muscles of his stomach and the trail of hair, so overtly sexual. What did he fantasize about? He had left his past, but there were things that couldn't be buried. Was there a part of him that still craved something rougher? A part of him he had lulled to sleep in his new, reformed life? Did I dare try to awaken that part again?

I swallowed. I could nudge him right now and ask. But he might not know the answer. After all, I thought I had left guys like this behind years ago until Jonas showed up. If I wanted to know, I'd have to find out for myself.

Jonas shifted, his muscles flexing with each movement. There were so many ways I could wake him up. Though a shower should probably come first. I sighed and headed for the bathroom.

Showering was more complicated than it sounded. The tub was the old-fashioned kind that rested on four, elegant feet with ornate fixtures. Made for baths. Missing was the curtain. The shower head wrapped around the faucet. Apparently, I was supposed to hold it in one hand and wash myself with the other, all without soaking the 100-plus-year-old walls around me. Right.

At least it was warm out. How did anyone shower in the wintertime in this place?

I turned the hot and cold knobs and peeled off my travel clothes. I tested the temperature and stepped into the tub. I let out a sigh as the warm water ran over my body. How I would manage soap at the same time was still a mystery, but for now, I closed my eyes and let the heat flow over me.

My eyes snapped open at the sound of the doorknob. I turned my head. Jonas leaned in the doorway, watching me. He had taken off his shirt, exposing the rest of his stomach and the broad muscles of his chest. His lips were parted again, and a hint of a smile teased at the corners of his mouth. But his eyes held a darker hunger of the most basic kind. The kind that got my imagination going.

He reached down to adjust the bulge in his pants, his tattoos rippling with each move. I traced each muscle with my eyes, slowly, deliberately. He was mine for the next twenty-four hours, and I was going to make this the best twenty-four hours of my life.

His intense blue eyes hinted at something darker. His past, his book, his scarred body suggested something rougher. Something dangerous. Something that turned my insides to flames, whether or not I liked it.

My breasts were heavy, and I cupped one with my hand. I teased my nipple, sending a shot of pleasure through my core. Jonas's eyes widened, his hand still on his erection.

I raised an eyebrow. "*S'il vous plait?*"

At the sound of my voice, some of the darkness lifted from his gaze. He smiled. "Can I help you with your shower?"

His voice was still rough with sleep, and he ran a hand through his tousled hair, waiting for my reply. I teased my nipple again and nodded at Jonas. Then I turned my back to him.

Closing my eyes, I let my other senses take over. Warm streams of water. The rustle of his jeans falling to the floor. The brush of my thumb over my nipple. His footsteps, closer.

His hand rested low on my hip as he stepped into the tub. He lifted my hair and kissed my shoulder, tasting my skin with his tongue. His teeth scraped the side of my neck. My breath caught in my throat. He pressed his chest against my back and slid his erection between my legs.

"Repeat after me," Jonas whispered, letting his lips linger on my earlobe. "*Lave-moi, s'il vous plait.*"

"*Lave-moi, s'il vous plait,*" I echoed.

"*Tres bien.* Very good."

He found the drain plug and let the water fill the tub. His hands explored my stomach and fondled my breasts as the water splashed at our ankles. Jonas took the showerhead from me and turned off the water. He sat down, sprawling across the tub, his legs open. Heat pulsed through me as I pictured where this was leading.

"Now come and straddle me," he said, his voice rumbling in his throat.

I held onto the sides of the tub and lowered myself to kneel over him. I shifted forward, and my breasts brushed against him. His breath stopped, but he didn't move. He kept his gaze steady on my face as I balanced myself over him.

"I don't think condoms work well in the water," he said, his voice tight. "But we can do other things."

I nodded a little. Other things. What kinds of other things filled his fantasies? Darker things that he had written about in his book?

His hands caressed my hips as he guided me over the top of his hard, full length. He shifted to raise his knees. His gaze still fixed on me, he thrust, sliding along my core.

I squeezed my eyes closed at the intense pleasure and let out a soft cry. His erection jerked under me, setting off another rush of intense heat that echoed through me. He smiled a little. His short, raspy breaths rang in my ears.

"Are you ready for the soap?" he whispered.

I opened my eyes and looked into the deep blue of his gaze. "I assumed we were skipping that part when you climbed into the tub with me."

Jonas shook his head. "Oh no. I just didn't want you to get bored."

"Very generous of you."

Our breaths and little laughs echoed in the room.

"But you'll have to keep still, or this will all be over much sooner than either of us would like," he said. He leaned forward, and his lips tasted the base of my neck. "*Le savon, s'il vous plait*? The soap."

I turned to the shelf behind me and reached for the soap. I shifted, trying out a new position against his hard length. I stretched over him, and he leaned forward to catch my breast in his mouth.

"Oh, God," I moaned.

He let go and settled back against the tub, his breaths coming faster. The soap. Right. Jonas's eyes were closed. I lifted one of his hands off my hips and set the little bar in it. Then I leaned forward to touch my lips to his, letting the tips of my breasts brush against his chest.

I sighed. "I'm ready."

A string of foreign words came out in his harsh breath. He opened his eyes again and gave me a hazy smile. I shifted back, and a shudder ran through his body, triggering my own.

He lathered the soap and moved his hand slowly up and down one of my arms. I opened my mouth to comment on my own imperfections, but the intensity in Jonas's gaze made me hold back. Instead, I leaned forward and kissed him softly.

What would it be like to have him inside me right now? To throw away all caution and for once just do what I wanted to do? And where would that push him?

He moved to focus on my other arm. His body twitched and flexed under his movements, but he took his time. He studied each part of my body as he worked his way down, over my breasts, and along the curves of my stomach and hips. Neither of us spoke.

When he had worked his way down my body, he turned on the showerhead to rinse me off. Trails of water ran down my body and over his.

"When I was a teenager, I used to get myself off to fantasies like this," he groaned.

I smiled. "I bet you were an interesting teenager."

"That's a polite way of saying it." His eyes were serious for a moment, but he shook his head, and the look was gone.

I took the showerhead from him and set it aside. "Is it my turn now?"

Jonas's eyes widened, and he shifted his hips against mine.

"Whatever you'd like," he whispered.

I kissed him softly and reached for the soap. My hands glided over the warm, smooth muscles of his chest and shoulders. I studied his tattoos, tracing the lines of unrecognizable words. I rested my fingers on the large black bird with the injured wing. He didn't flinch, but his breaths came quicker. Was that him, broken, flying away from it all? I looked up, my question on my lips, but his eyes were far away.

No. I wasn't going to push him. Not here, not now. I dropped my eyes to the tattoo on his shoulders, following the design over the bulk of his arm.

"When did you get this one?" I asked, touching the ends of the faded, tribal-like design.

"Right when I turned eighteen," he said. "I was tall, but I hadn't filled out much yet. I had started fighting a little, and I wanted to intimidate the guys I was up against. Not sure if it worked." He gave me a wry smile.

My fingers stopped, and I looked up at him again. "What kind of fighting?"

Jonas frowned. "For money. Nothing legal."

I waited for more, but he didn't say anything more.

"Any regrets about the tattoo now that you're not in the intimidation business anymore?" I asked.

"Don't really think about it anymore." Jonas's expression softened, and he chuckled. "Why? You don't like tattoos?"

The heat traveled up my neck. "I do. I wish they didn't turn me on, but they do."

He looked at me, brow furrowed, but I wasn't in the mood to talk more about that. Not when there were so many other things I wanted to do right now.

I placed the soap back into the tray and continued my explorations. Jonas closed his eyes. I ran my hand over his neck, and his pulse pounded under my fingertips. His hands pressed against my thighs, and his thumbs circled higher.

I found the showerhead and rinsed him off. The water ran down his chest and steamed from the pool in the tub. I turned off the knobs.

"Fuck, this feels good," he growled, his hands clenching as he thrust his hips.

He cupped my cheeks and brought his lips to mine. I reached between us and gave his erection a hard stroke. Jonas gritted his teeth and tipped his head back. Before I could think through my next move, I rose up and positioned him at my entrance.

"Are you clean?" I whispered.

He nodded a little, his eyes shut.

In one slick move, I lowered myself over his thick, throbbing length. I shuddered, pleasure and relief flowing through me. I wanted to be closer, even closer. His skin against mine. My body contracted. This was heaven, just Jonas and me and nothing else. If I just did that a couple more times—

"Shit," Jonas bit out. "We can't do this, *Alice*."

My body begged for just one more delicious thrust. I drew in a shaky breath and stilled myself. Damn. What the hell was I thinking? I rose up until I released him.

"That's hot as hell," he rasped. "But if we're going bare, we need to be ready to look way past tomorrow."

I squeezed my eyes shut and nodded. I rested my forehead against his chest and felt the hard, fast thump of his heart.

"Should we get out and find a condom?" he asked, his voice rumbling in his chest.

I nodded again, trying to get a handle on my thoughts. I couldn't forget for one moment that we only had one more night. Then I was leaving. The end.

I climbed out of the tub and grabbed a towel. Splashes came from behind me, and I turned to see Jonas rising out of the water, like some Viking god, water running in streaks down his tattooed chest. And a thick, erection bobbing impatiently at me. He was staring at my ass with dark hunger that sent a fire through my insides. Oh, God. What was he imagining?

But as I turned, his expression went blank. Yet another part of him that he kept carefully locked up?

I handed Jonas a towel. He dried off carelessly, missing beads of water on his thick biceps and his powerful shoulders. Dropping my towel, I stepped closer and licked the water from his skin. I tasted the intricate weavings of the Celtic cross, moving, higher. Then I raised myself onto my toes and rested my lips against the broken wing of the black bird.

He let out a groan of unmistakable pleasure. Yes, he really liked that. He was a man who willingly fought, and if his scars were any indication, he didn't always win.

But my imagination wouldn't stop there. What did he want afterward with his red-headed girlfriend? An unbidden image came: Jonas holding down another woman. He wouldn't have been as gentle and controlled with that woman as he was with me. Jealousy flashed through me, sudden and unexpected.

I looked up at him and traced the scar on his jaw. "Do you ever miss being a little rougher?"

He froze, his muscles tensed. "I don't miss the fighting."

"That's not what I mean," I whispered.

His chest rose and fell against me.

"I know," he said slowly. "But I don't know the answer to your question. The fighting, the drugs, the sex – for me it's all wrapped up together. And I'm not sure I want to sort it out."

This was an answer. His uncertainty. Still so wary of his past, of what he was capable of. He wanted something different, but that didn't mean his taste for rougher things was gone.

I looked up at him. "What do you really want to do with me right now, Jonas?"

He parted his mouth as if to speak, but he stopped. He caught my lip between his teeth, and I moaned. He kissed me again as we took slow steps out of the bathroom and toward the bed.

"I'll show you," he said.

My heart stuttered as the backs of my legs hit the bed.

"You want to know what I want right now?" His lips brushed mine as he spoke.

I shook my head slowly.

"I want to be the man who makes you come with my mouth. I want you to straddle me and tease me while I do it. And then I want to lose myself with you."

A rush of pleasure pulsed from my core, and I drew in a shaky breath. Not exactly what I had been thinking. Not rough, not now. But wow. Definitely something new.

He held my face in his hands and whispered, "I want everything a selfish prick in jail can't have. Even if it's just for the night."

I blinked. His jaw was still tight. I kissed him softly on his scar, warmth washing through me. He was still running from his past just as hard as I was. But he knew where he wanted to go.

"What do you think, Alice?"

I swallowed. "*Si'l vous plait.*"

A little of the tension in his jaw eased, and his eyes softened. "Good."

My heart raced faster. I had never done anything like this before. I folded my arms, suddenly awkward.

"You don't have to be nervous," he said, stroking my cheek. "You'll like this."

He pulled back the covers and lay down. "Turn around and put your knees up around my shoulders. You can lean forward and play from there."

Heat blazed up my cheeks as I flashed to an image of lowering myself onto his mouth. Could I go through with this? I'd never have the nerve to ask for it. But this was *his* fantasy.

Clearly I needed to work on my own imagination.

I stepped closer and stopped. "Are you sure you want to do this?"

"Hell, yes." Jonas smiled, and his eyes darkened. "The night after you left for Copenhagen, I got myself off thinking about this."

I climbed onto the bed and braced myself on his chest as he helped position me. He held my hips steady over him. I looked up at his long, hard length, begging for attention.

"I'm hard as fuck right now," he groaned. "But I don't want to come. Not yet. So just play a little if you want. But not too much."

"Okay," I said, my voice quivering.

He tugged my hips, and I sank down onto his mouth.

"Ooohhh," I whispered.

The sensation of his mouth was overpowering as he tasted me, again and again. And then there was the view. I had never had the chance to stare at a man this way, and I probably never would again. I shifted my weight onto my hands for a closer look as he teased me.

I tried to focus on his throbbing erection in front of me. Did he really get off on giving my pleasure? Was this part of what he had said earlier about what he had missed in prison? The power and the intimacy in giving someone else pleasure were two things no one had behind bars.

I reached forward with one hand and touched his wet tip. His hips jolted, and his hard breaths whispered at my core. Jonas swept his tongue over a sensitive spot, and I cried out. He caressed my hips and did it again. It was getting hard to think, but I wasn't done exploring. I circled him with my hand, feeling his size and weight. He was rock hard, probably painfully so, but he had said he didn't want to come yet. I had never done anything this erotic before. And I had never been so turned on. He teased me with his mouth as I traced his length with my fingers.

I couldn't take it much longer.

With one more circle of his tongue, everything inside tightened and burst. Jonas held me in place, teasing out more jolts of ecstasy, and I collapsed on his hot stomach. I closed my eyes.

"My God," I mumbled.

The softer waves of pleasure echoed and faded, coaxing me into a languid haze. I rolled off him, and he turned around to face me.

"Wow," I whispered.

Jonas nodded. "Mmm."

"Just give me a minute," I panted.

Jonas chuckled. "I'll try."

He headed for the bathroom and returned with a glass of water. The bed dipped as he sat down on the edge. He took a drink and rubbed the back of his neck with his hand.

"I can't decide if this is so good because we just met or despite it," I said, tracing a thick line of his tattoo around his shoulders with my fingers.

He turned around and rested his hand on mine. "Doesn't matter," he said quietly. "It's a lonely world out there. Being with you makes it better. That's all that matters."

I swallowed. He was right. If nothing else, we had found a reprieve.

He reached for a condom on the night stand and scooted back on the bed. I climbed over his legs and straddled him. I took the condom from him and rolled it on. He lifted me and slowly I lowered myself. I was still so sensitive, and the pressure was almost too much.

"You okay?" he asked, teeth gritted.

I nodded.

"You make me hungry, Alice," he groaned. "Hungry for things I never thought I could have."

His words rang like a bell deep inside, echoing through my body.

Jonas rolled on top of me and laced our hands together, lifting them over my head. He kissed me as he began to move in long, slow thrusts. His hands grasped mine harder at every thrust and he bent down to open my mouth for a kiss. I felt the mounting pleasure pushing out the sadness. I tipped back my head, losing myself in the heat and the friction of Jonas's body. His eyes were heavy with pleasure, his lips parted. I didn't look away. His strokes grew harder, faster, more and more frantic.

The bed creaked and groaned under the weight of each thrust.

He reached his hand between my legs for a few soft swirls, sending my body to the brink of ecstasy. He bucked and growled and bucked until I screamed his name. I shook with pleasure as he drove in his final thrusts with heavy, torn groans. He came hard, his muscles straining and twitching. His head dropped to my neck, and he whispered words I couldn't understand.

But I didn't need to. Not when he clung to me like he'd never let me go.

4

THE SUN HAD shifted across the room. I lay half on top of Jonas, legs tangled, suspended in a dreamy, sated fog.

"I'm starving," said Jonas, stroking my hair.

He kissed me and sat up, the bed groaning under his movements.

I sat on the edge, watching him. His muscles stretched and flexed as he pulled on a white t-shirt. A dark beast of an inked creature slithered around his thick, hard bicep.

"When did you get that tattoo?" I asked.

He frowned. "Not long before I went to jail."

What was the beast? Its eyes were dark, and drops of blood hung from its teeth. Was it part of him? It must be if he marked his body permanently with it.

I bit my lip. How much should I push him to tell me more? He shut down every time parts of his past came up. The rest of his life wasn't supposed to matter, not when we had only a day together, but somehow it did.

He took out a crisp blue button-down shirt from his suitcase and slipped his arms through the sleeves, covering the tattoo.

I raised my eyebrows at him. "Are you dressing up for me?"

He looked up at me, and the distance in his eyes melted. "Can't think of a better reason than that."

My cheeks flushed. A lock of wet, tousled hair fell onto his forehead as he buttoned up his shirt. He looked up at me again, and I licked my lips. His eyes widen. He took a slow step forward and ran a hand down my bare arm.

I traced the buttons of his shirt. Kneeling down in front of me, he leaned in for a soft kiss.

"You look beautiful," he whispered, his voice warm and low in my ear. "Naked, your hair all tousled and wild."

He found my breast with his hand, and my breath caught in the back of my throat.

He took a long, deep breath. "Fuck, you smell good." He squeezed my breast and groaned, then let go. "You better get some clothes on." He handed me the sundress that I had hung over the chair in the corner.

How could this be the same man who covered his body with dark ink? A girl could get hooked on the kinds of complements that slipped out of his mouth. He must have gotten burned for laying himself out like this before, and yet he still did it.

But he was careful with some parts, and some parts he seemed to have closed off completely. Or tried to. What would I find if I pushed him a little more? Sometime today, I was going to find out.

I touched his cheek with my fingertips. "You're a remarkable man, Jonas Hällström."

He looked at me, his eyes flickering with unreadable emotion, but he didn't say anything.

We rode the elevator down to the lobby in silence, my fingers laced with his. We walked out onto the little square. I hadn't noticed the rain shower from the room, but the sidewalk was damp. I breathed in the warm, soft air and sighed aloud. Jonas grinned down at me and squeezed my hand.

We crossed onto a larger boulevard. The sidewalks were filled with people, though no one seemed to be in much of a hurry. Jonas and I joined the stream of Parisians, passing hat shops and chocolatiers. A man in an apron was wiping down the wicker-backed chairs and tiny tables of a café's outdoor seating.

Jonas peeked into the first bakery we came to. The smell of butter and yeast wafted from the narrow store. My stomach rumbled.

Jonas looked down at his watch. "It's a little early for dinner. Maybe something from here?"

I took a long drag of the sweet smells. "Mmm. If I step into that bakery, I'm afraid of how much I'll come out with."

Jonas raised an eyebrow "Is that a bad thing?"

"I think so," I said. "This trip is eroding all my self-control."

Jonas bent down and kissed my neck. "Lucky me. You want to wait outside? I'll surprise you."

I nodded. He brushed his hand over my cheek and turned for the door.

I chose the table next to the window and leaned back into the chair. A little vase of purple and yellow pansies sat on a square of linen on the side of the table, along with a menu, handwritten in calligraphy. Someone had spent time on this beautiful arrangement, protected it from the rain.

I looked through the window of the café for Jonas. His broad back was to me, his hands shoved in his pockets. The cashier pointed at a pastry, and Jonas nodded.

He looked like the last guy I'd expect to find on the Paris streets, but he didn't seem to notice. Or maybe he just didn't care. Even all dressed up, he still radiated *don't fuck with me.*

Where I grew up, a guy like him would have ruled the neighborhood. He would have had a girlfriend he took out plus a few more on the side. If he wasn't in jail. Or dead. I frowned. Thoughts like that didn't belong in this Paris fantasy.

Jonas returned with a tray and set it on the little table. The scents of coffee and butter mingled in the warm air.

I sighed. "Coffee this late in the day?"

"So we'll stay up all night," he said. "I'm helping you get back on New York time."

I rolled my eyes. "*Merci.*"

"Nice French."

"And I figured it out all by myself."

Jonas's mouth twisted up in a smile. "We can stay up late for more French lessons."

"You still haven't taught me any dirty words."

"Are we making a list of things we haven't done yet?" Jonas's hand disappeared under the table and slipped up my thigh. "I have a few things to add."

I laughed. "You've definitely done that before."

Jonas set a frothy cup in front of me, and he took the black coffee for himself. I took a sip of the creamy drink and bit into the fluffy croissant. I closed my eyes, concentrating on the buttery pastry flakes melting in my mouth. Jonas's hand was gone, but his thigh pressed against mine, warm, solid. The sun shone on my back, and the warmth spread through me.

Would I remember this feeling when I got back to New York?

I opened my eyes as Jonas took the last bite of his croissant. Leaning forward over the table, he lifted a hand to my cheek. I took a stuttered breath. He opened his mouth as if to speak, but only his breath came out.

He shook his head a little and dropped his hand. "Ready?"

I nodded.

We wandered slowly down the street, dodging dogs, well-dressed men and mysteriously well-composed children. The sun shone down on the damp pavement, and a hint of mist rose in front of us. Jonas slipped his arm around my waist and pointed to a narrow side street, away from the crowded boulevard.

We crossed, his long strides slowing to match my pace. I slowed further in front of a narrow arching entrance to a bookstore. The front windows were blocked on both sides with teetering stacks of books. Mismatched tables on the sidewalk held wicker baskets, all overflowing with more books. I stopped next to one of the tables and ran my fingers along the spines.

Jonas picked up a yellowing paperback and flipped through the first pages. I scanned the table for a familiar name. Jean-Paul Sartre. I picked up the book and looked at the cover. A few words in French and the name Simone de Beauvoir. Jonas put his book down and looked over my shoulder.

"Sartre's love letters to de Beauvoir in French?" he asked. I could hear the smile in his voice. "Ambitious."

I laughed. "I'm not going to buy it. Just recognized the names."

He brushed his hand over my shoulder, along my shoulder blades. "Live for the moment, right?"

"Always." I rolled my eyes. Though living for the moment was going pretty well so far. Must be the magic of Paris at work.

"Why publishing, Alice?" asked Jonas. "You're... unexpected."

"That's coming from you?"

"That's fair." He laughed, and his low voice hummed through me. "But why?"

I shrugged. "Books got me through a lot of years. Probably a good thing since most of my friends ended up pregnant. Mostly it was just my mother and me in a one-bedroom apartment. We had no money. The only people who had money in my neighborhood were trouble."

I glanced up at him, and he raised an eyebrow. "You should stay away from that kind of trouble," he said.

The corners of my mouth pulled up. He had been that kind of trouble, too.

"I try to. But it finds me anyway, apparently," I said.

He laughed, and we started walking again. He kept his eyes on me, waiting for me to continue.

I sighed. "All I wanted was to not end up like my mother. She drilled it into me from a young age that I needed a good man to take care of me. She spent her life pining after my father, but he was in and out of jail." I glanced over at Jonas. "Not sure if she thought he was one of those 'good men' or not."

I hadn't talked about any of this in a long time. I had worked hard to mellow out my Brooklyn accent, and by the end of my freshman year at Columbia, my background rarely came up. It was strange to think about my teenage years on this Paris street, but Jonas was watching me, his face carefully neutral, waiting for me to continue. What else was there to say?

I stopped in the window of a jewelry store, feigning interest in a display of earrings. I took a deep breath. "My mother also thought college was a waste of money. My college admissions essay and my English teacher's recommendation got me a scholarship, so she stopped bothering me about it. And I was suddenly an English major. Publishing was about as far from my neighborhood as I could get, so I went for it."

My own voice sounded hollow. I shouldn't have even brought up my mother. All those things were in the past, and there was nothing else to do but move ahead.

I waited in front of the sets of wispy silver earrings, bracing myself for more questions about my past, but they didn't come. I really liked this about him, that he didn't press me too much.

He looked at the jewelry display in front of me. "Which ones?"

There were larger and smaller versions of interwoven silver threads, all delicate and beautiful. I pointed at the pair at the end, long and extravagant. "Those."

He smiled. "You want them?"

Was he offering to buy me jewelry? Probably not.

I shook my head. "I've already—" I caught myself before I finished the sentence. I had already spent too much money.

"No, thanks," I finished.

He waited for an extra beat, then let that go, too.

Jonas took my hand, and we walked slowly along the street. I closed my eyes and breathed in the sweet, full scent of chocolate wafting out of the shop we passed.

"It's been a long, long time since I've just wandered around," I said.

"No walks in Central Park with that boyfriend of yours?"

I snorted. "Hardly. He wasn't the type."

"What type is that?"

I could hear the smile in his voice. I shrugged. "You know, flowers and balloons and mushy crap like that."

Jonas laughed. "I'll be careful not to try any of that *crap* on you."

I glanced up at him and raised an eyebrow. "Oh yeah? What kinds of things are we talking about?"

"Wouldn't you like to know." He feigned interest in the window display of men's shirts, but I could see the smile on his face grow broader. "Probably too mushy for your refined tastes."

"Probably," I said, biting back my own smile.

"So what was he like?" asked Jonas.

"Who? Neil?"

"That's your ex-boyfriend's name?" He smirked. "He sounds short and wimpy."

I laughed. "Nah, not really."

"Did he wear a suit?"

I nodded. "Sure. Typical executive wear, I guess."

Jonas stopped walking and turned to me.

"He's an executive?" he asked.

"Yes. At Boars and Allen."

Jonas's eyes widened. "You work with him?"

I squirmed under his stare, regretting my last comment. I really didn't want to talk about this.

"A little," I said. "He's not my boss, if that's what you're wondering."

Jonas didn't say anything. We walked, neither speaking. Finally, he stopped and turned to me.

"Were you in love?"

"No," I said. "Not even close."

I had surprised both Neil and myself by simply saying no when he asked me to move in with him. And thank God I did. After that, it was as if he had saved all his nastiest thoughts in the unlikely event that I turned him down.

"Have you ever been in love?"

I looked away and shook my head. I probably wasn't the type who could really, truly fall in love.

But before I could take another step, he threw his arms around me and picked me up.

"Someday, Alice," he whispered. "Someday."

He put me down and held my face in his hands. His lips met mine, lingering. *Someday* wasn't a consolation. *Someday* was a promise. One that he couldn't make. So why was my heart thumping so hard?

I started down the street again "Why the interest in Neil? Believe me, it's a lot less dramatic than it sounds."

Jonas slipped his arm around my waist, and we fell into step.

"I'm just trying to figure you out," he said. "It feels good to wonder, to discover things about you. I've never really had a normal, get-to-know-you relationship."

"I guess I get it," I said, slowing. "But we don't have a relationship."

"We do right now," he said giving me a pointed look. "So I'm acting like it right now."

I furrowed my brow.

Jonas looked down at me, and his expression was serious. "We don't know what will happen next. Anything's possible. What if you get hit by one of these crazy taxis on the next corner? Then I definitely won't regret asking you any of these things."

I blinked. "Hmm. That's deep, Jonas."

The corners of his eyes crinkled, and he chuckled. "Don't worry. I'm usually much shallower."

I smiled a little. Always so self-deprecating. But a humble man wouldn't make it in the intimidation business. He had another side, one that was written all over his body in ink. One that he kept far away from me. When did it come out? All it took for my father to flip was a few late nights.

Damn. Why the hell was I thinking about my father again? Jonas wasn't like him, not now anyway. And our "relationship" had less than a day left. I slipped my arms around his waist, searching for the warmth of his body against my hands. Neither of us spoke. We walked under the awnings of a row of stores rippling in the soft breeze.

"If I get a contract with a U.S. publisher for this book, I'll probably come to New York," said Jonas. "I just wanted to put that out there."

He said it offhandedly, as if he were mentioning the weather.

"Oh." What was he expecting me to say? That my heart pounded wildly at the idea of seeing him again? It was. I took a deep breath and kept my expression blank.

"It's just that I'm an asshole in real life," he said. "I don't want you to see me that way."

I took more slow, even breaths. Maybe I had been wrong. Maybe he did have a lot in common with my father.

I let go of his waist and bent down to adjust my shoe. I wasn't going to let him see any hint of disappointment on my face. This shouldn't be a surprise, so why did I feel the sting of rejection? I should be relieved. Knowing that the end was near, there was no reason to hold back. I could be selfish, ask whatever I wanted of him tonight. Not worry whether I was pushing him too far. I straightened up again.

We turned down another narrow street, one without stores, only quiet doorways to the old buildings that rose up in shades of greys and tans. Jonas and I were the only ones on the street, our footsteps the only sounds above the din of traffic in the background.

We cut around one corner and another until we came to the enormous boulevard where the taxi had dropped us off. Across it, beyond the low concrete wall, I caught a glimpse of the Seine. In the distance, and around the river's bend, the Eiffel Tower rose up through the trees.

This was it. The Paris of my dreams. A rush of giddy excitement ran through me, pushing away the sullen thoughts about Jonas. I was here, right now, with a man who could turn me on with a few whispered words. And he did, over and over again. That was enough, wasn't it?

"Let's cross over," I said. "I want to get closer to the river."

The sun had disappeared behind a stack of puffy clouds, and the water of the Seine glimmered in purples and blues. We found the wide path that took us down below street level, along the river's curves. The concrete bank sloped down into the water, and a few men and women sat along the edge, some in groups, some alone, reading or smoking cigarettes or just talking. We passed a couple deep in a kiss. One of the man's hands slid up the young woman's leg, under her skirt. I stared as they passed by, but neither the man nor the woman noticed. The woman moaned like she didn't care who stared or heard her. How far would they go out here on the banks of the Seine?

Jonas squeezed my hand and nodded toward the couple. "Want to try that?"

I shook my head. "I'm not into making out in public."

"We haven't done that yet?" he asked, slowing to a stop. "A bedroom kiss out in the open?"

"Just that kiss on the Stockholm street, but no one was around."

His eyes turned hungry. Was he remembering that kiss, too? His lips parted. "Hmm… I hadn't thought about it, but maybe we haven't." He raised an eyebrow. "You never got a little tipsy and made out with your ex-boyfriend on the subway platform?"

I snorted. "I doubt Neil has ever taken the subway. But no." I tried to imagine a kiss right there in the street with Jonas as his hands explored more intimate places. I frowned. The idea was more embarrassing than sexy. "I think I'd just feel like I'm showing off. Like it's for other people, not me."

"Even here, in a foreign country?"

"I don't know." I studied the others wandering by. No one else seemed to be paying much attention to the amorous couple. The woman had shifted onto the man's lap.

"No one seems to care," I said. "Maybe I'd be okay, but I still don't get why someone would want to."

Jonas's eyes crinkled at the corners, but he suppressed his smile. "Maybe they get caught up in the moment?"

"I guess." I shrugged.

He laughed and started walking again.

I arched an eyebrow at him. "Are you laughing at me?"

"Never."

I gave him a little shove. "There goes the romantic walk by the Seine."

Jonas glanced at his watch. "Then let's eat. I know a great place around here." He planted a wet, showy kiss on my lips. He pulled back, and his face glowed with amusement.

I shook my head and smiled a little. Not bad.

We crossed the busy boulevard and headed to another little street. Jonas looked so at ease. Was he happy? Maybe. Now that he had cleared up our non-existent future.

The lights inside the shops glowed. We walked closer, dodging other couples on the narrow sidewalk, and my hand brushed against his, intimate, his body so close.

Jonas stopped outside one of the restaurants. The menu was written in elegant script on a giant chalkboard next to the doorway—in French, of course. At least the prices were clear. At second glance, that wasn't a good thing. Everything was too expensive. Even the very first item, which was probably some tiny arrangement of lettuce leaves. My stomach growled, begging for more than just lettuce.

Damn. In the whirlwind of my day with Jonas, I had almost succeeded in forgetting about this most basic problem. I couldn't really afford this trip. Stockholm and Copenhagen were paid for by Boars and Allen. Here, I was on my own. If I spent this kind of money on dinner, I'd probably max my overcharged credit card before I even saw the hotel bill. Did they have vending machines in Paris?

I swallowed and turned to Jonas. "Um, on second thought, maybe we can just grab a sandwich from the bakery we passed and head to the hotel."

The heat crept up the back of my neck, and I looked away. Maybe he'd think it was a play to get him back into bed.

He said nothing. Finally, I glanced back up at him.

Jonas was studying me, brow furrowed. "Would it help if I read the menu to you?"

His eyes searched mine. If I were standing here with Neil, this discussion would have already turned into an argument about how I never just let go. How if I just relaxed a little, I'd be more fun. But Jonas wasn't Neil, not even close.

Lie to Jonas or spend money I really, really didn't have? My morals were eroding by the minute. I had to think of something, but exhaustion and hunger were setting in.

"Sure. Let's go in, and you can read me the menu," I said.

It took a moment for my eyes to adjust to the small, candlelit place with low ceilings. The tables were packed together, leaving little room to maneuver, and the dark, wooden walls were filled with old photographs and signs. Jazz played softly in the background. One other couple sat at a table next to the window, leaning together, their faces glowing in the evening light.

Jonas said something in French to the waiter and motioned to the back corner table. The waiter nodded and led us through the restaurant. I chose the bench seat by the wall, and the waiter handed me a menu. I searched for something recognizable.

"Escargot?" I read.

Jonas's face lit up. "Want to try it?"

I looked up and wrinkled my nose. "Snails, right? Hmm…"

"It'll be a first for me," said Jonas. "I'll order it."

I scanned my menu and set it down. "Just order something French for me."

"This is all French," he said dryly.

I rolled my eyes. "I mean something typically French. Something unforgettable."

"You're setting the bar high. I'll try to deliver."

The waiter returned, and Jonas spoke with him for a few moments, gesturing. The man took our menus, and walked away.

"I ordered you the beef bourguignon and a glass of wine," said Jonas. "Not fancy but definitely French."

"Thanks."

Jonas slid a hand under the little table and rested it on my knee. A crease had formed between his eyebrows, but he didn't say anything.

I had so many questions for him.

"You're accent sounds Scottish or Irish," I tried.

"I spent some time in Dublin."

"Why Dublin?"

"It was a good place to earn money." Jonas hesitated, then added, "And there was a woman."

I raised an eyebrow. "A red-haired woman?"

Jonas nodded slowly. "Yes."

The image of Jonas and another woman came before I could stop it. His hands in her hair as he kissed her. His big, hard body over hers as his face twisted in pleasure. I frowned.

"Did you love her?" I asked.

Jonas turned his head to the row of empty tables next to us and sighed. "I don't know. Sometimes I thought I did, but I thought a lot of crazy things back then."

My heart pounded in my chest.

"Why did you two break up?"

"We fought a lot. After a while it was just fighting. And sex. By the end, the sex felt a lot like fighting, too." Jonas's expression was unreadable.

Sex and fighting. What would that be like with Jonas? Despite his size, he hadn't tried anything... intimidating in bed. Far from it. Far from anything I'd expect from a man who would land in prison.

I tucked a lock of hair behind my ear. If I wanted to know about his past, now was the time to ask.

"Was she the one you were in Paris with?"

Jonas nodded.

"The woman from your novel?"

Jonas shrugged. "Some parts."

"You said the character in your novel is American, not Irish," I said.

"True. Let's just say that I rewrote my own history in the book."

He didn't offer anything more. Now I really did need to read his book, though it was probably better if he wasn't around for it.

"I've never had sex with someone I was fighting with," I said.

"What happened when you and Neil were ending things?"

"We just didn't have sex," I said. "He said I was too cold to be sexy."

Jonas muttered a few words under his breath and shook his head. "Sounds like a real fucker to me."

"Yeah, he is," I said. "But it took a while for that side to come out."

I blinked away the unexpected tears at the corners of my eyes. Why the hell did I care about what Neil thought?

"He really hurt you," he said softly. "What else did he say?"

My cheeks burned. I hadn't repeated Neil's last words to anyone. But why the hell shouldn't I?

"He said that women like me end up alone."

Jonas's face flushed an angry red. "What the fuck does that mean?"

I swallowed hard.

"I don't know," I whispered. "He asked me to move in with him, maybe even get married someday, and I turned him down. That's when all this started."

Jonas watched me, his face still flushed, his pulse pumping at the base of his neck. I studied his face, looking for some hint at what he was thinking, but he gave nothing away. Jonas wouldn't say the kinds of things that came out of Neil's mouth after that awful dinner, but did he think any of them? Not that it mattered.

"Do you want to get married someday?" he asked softly.

He didn't mean with him. So why was my stupid heart pounding again?

I forced a little smile. "I'm not sure I'm the type."

Jonas nodded.

The waiter brought me a glass of wine and a glass of water for Jonas.

"No wine for you?" I asked.

"No," he said. "I don't usually drink much. Probably best for everyone."

He took a long gulp from his water glass. I shifted in my seat, and our knees brushed underneath the small table.

Jonas lifted his eyes, and they were filled with heat and anger. "If I ever meet Neil, I'm going to want to punch that asshole in the face."

My heart sped up as I pictured the scene. Neil, in his suit on the Sixth Avenue sidewalk, who hadn't seen it coming. And Jonas by my side. This shouldn't have felt as good as it did.

5

WHEN I RETURNED from the restroom, the plates were cleared from the table.

Jonas was staring out the window, his brow furrowed. I slipped back into my chair, and the faraway look on his face disappeared. He smiled, the corners of his eyes crinkling. God, he was beautiful.

"What's next this evening?" he asked.

I glanced around the little restaurant. Guests were beginning to trickle in, but the tables next to us were still empty. I sipped the last of my wine and took a deep breath. No more holding back.

"You promised me some bedroom French," I said.

His eyes darkened. "And you want that now?"

I nodded.

"What do you want to learn?" His voice was lower, deeper.

I leaned closer. "How do I say *fuck me*?"

He closed his eyes and swallowed. "*Baise-moi.*"

"*Baise-moi,*" I repeated. Then I whispered it again. "*Baise-moi.*"

My heart was doing strange things, fluttering and pounding as he opened his eyes. His gaze turned hotter, hungrier.

"What else do you want to learn?" he groaned.

I hesitated. But why? This was my chance to explore. To be free.

"How do you say *suck my cock*?"

"*Suce-moi la bite.*" Jonas hissed out a breath, then laughed. "Are you going to repeat that?"

104

"No." I smiled. "I just want to understand when you say it to me."

He muttered something incomprehensible and reached a hand under the table. Was this getting him hard? Good. But I wasn't done.

"And *swallow*?" I whispered, drawing out the word. "How do you say *swallow*?"

Jonas's gaze exploded with lust. "*Avale*, Alice," he bit out. "*Avale*."

I pushed back my chair and stood up. "Ready?"

Jonas laughed darkly. "You're good, Alice."

AS WE NEARED the Eiffel Tower, the cab driver turned, heading away from the river. I glanced at Jonas. The bulge in his pants wasn't as noticeable anymore, but the electricity between us still sizzled high.

At this time tomorrow, Jonas would be on a plane back to Stockholm, and I would be somewhere over the Atlantic. On Monday morning I would walk back into the office and hand my boss the translation of the first chapter of Jonas's book as if it were any other story I had picked up from the Stockholm Book Expo. I'd tell no one about why I had rebooked my flight. It would all just disappear.

I would sit through meetings debating which books best fit the Boars and Allen list. And this night, one of the best nights in my life, would feel as if it belonged to someone else.

Jonas pulled me in closer, against his solid chest. The heat of his body seeped through the thin layers of clothing. We had no future, but if I could lose myself in the infinite now, maybe tomorrow it wouldn't feel like a mistake. One more night.

The taxi pulled over in front of a large stone building, and I opened the door into the night air. In the course of the cab ride, the sky had darkened. Wisps of purple clouds trailed across the deep red of the setting sun. The night air blew warm and heavy.

Jonas paid for the cab, and I didn't argue. He said something to the driver in French and joined me, slipping his large, warm hand into mine. The Eiffel Tower was nowhere in sight.

We crossed the street and walked toward the steps between two long stone buildings. Other couples wandered on the walkway above, and the night sky shone behind us. Jonas and I were half way up the steps when I saw why we had come here. In front of us, rising up just beyond the open plaza where the steps led, the Eiffel Tower appeared, lined with lights.

"Oh," I whispered.

"Amazing, right?"

"Amazing," I breathed. "I've seen tons of photos of the Eiffel Tower, but seeing it up close at night is something special."

Our shoes clicked on the steps.

"Did I thank you for dinner?" I asked. "You didn't have to pay, you know."

He stopped and turned to me. "We don't have much time left, *Alice*. I want to take you out, pretend you're my girlfriend for a little longer."

Before I could make sense of his comment, he kissed me. He pressed his lips to mine and slipped his other hand around the back of my neck. His breath was warm on my face, and he held me for an extra beat. It wasn't a bedroom kiss. It was almost as if he were saying goodbye.

I swallowed back the lump in my throat and searched for something to say. "So how do you afford this kind of thing? Does your family have money?"

"Not even close," he said. "I get it from my books."

I raised my eyebrows. "Most writers have a hard time making ends meet."

Jonas laughed. "I write a lot of books, and don't have much to spend money on. I live in a little one-bedroom apartment a few blocks away from the pub where we met, and I don't get out much."

"But you make enough to fly off to Paris on two days' notice."

"Maybe I'll have to pass up all other offers for weekends in Paris with hot women for a while."

Oh. I tried to smile.

His eyes widened, and he stopped. His face turned serious. "There aren't other weekends in Paris for me, Alice. I thought I made that clear. I spend most of my days alone. It's better that way."

It's better that way? It was the second time he had used that phrase. Was he living out his own, self-inflicted sentence? Was this why he had so bluntly ruled out seeing each other in New York?

I closed my eyes. No wonder my mother couldn't say no to my father. My parents had known each other for most of their lives. I had only met Jonas two days ago, and already I wanted to save him. To take him away from the past. To go back to the hotel and play out his fantasies. And lose myself in my own fantasy that a man like Jonas could bring more than heartache.

I met his gaze and smiled a little. "The Eiffel Tower is calling me."

Our footsteps echoed over the open plaza as more of the enormous tower came into sight. I slowed my steps, making each new view last longer. We crossed the plaza, along the wide path between two, mirroring buildings to the top of a long stretch of steps, heading downward. At the bottom of the staircase, a long pool of water stretched out toward the Eiffel Tower. The pool was broken up by symmetrical fountains, each spray lit up against the coming darkness of the evening. The noise of the city was dulled by the buildings that wrapped around behind us.

Jonas slipped his hands around my waist, and I let my body rest against his large chest as we gazed out at the city in front of us.

Another couple passed us on the steps, arm in arm. The man whispering in the woman's ear, and she laughed and kissed him. Back in New York, I tried to ignore couples like this. Happy couples. That just wasn't in the cards for me. But tonight it could be. I looked up at Jonas, his face glowing in all the lights.

"This is magical, Jonas," I whispered. Magical enough to make the impossible feel possible.

Jonas took one step lower and turned to me. He was still taller than me but only by a little. He caressed my cheek with the backs of his fingers. He tasted my lips, so softly, with all the longing and awareness of the clock that was ticking closer and closer to the end. He tasted again and again until I closed my eyes and tangled my hands in his hair, pulling him closer. He was everywhere against me, filling my senses, and still I couldn't get close enough. His tongue swept against mine, caressing, inviting. He pulled me so tightly, lifting me to further join our bodies, and I tilted my hips into his hard erection.

Oh, God. This was about to burst out of control, right here on the steps down to the Eiffel Tower. I broke off the kiss. The sound of my harsh breaths mingled with the city behind us. He buried his face in my neck, and I breathed in the scent of him. How could a man smell so good?

Slowly, the rest of the world came into focus.

"Wow," said Jonas, his voice rough. "Getting a taste for public affection?"

I smiled. "For tonight. One more night, right?"

"One more night," he echoed.

6

THE HOTEL ROOM glowed in the city lights. My body hummed in awareness as I opened the French doors to the little balcony. The cool night air rushed in.

I turned to Jonas, and he brushed the curls from my face. His thumb traced my skin.

"So this is it," I said softly. "This last night in Paris, and then it's over."

Jonas frowned and looked away. "It has to be."

But what if I came back to the Stockholm Book Expo? My mind clamored for an exception, a way to avoid the finality of our goodbye. But I wouldn't cross any more of my own hard limits. I wouldn't beg to see him again. Never.

I searched for something less desperate to say.

"What if Boars and Allen buys your book?" I asked. "What if you come to my office? What do we do?"

He grimaced, as if the idea caused him physical pain. But before I could react, he slipped his hand down my neck and pulled my closer. He buried his face in my hair.

"After you read my book, you won't want anything to do with me," he whispered. "So let's make this night last."

His words echoed in the dark room. Was it true? How bad would the story have to be to keep me away? And did he mean that what he wrote was real? He wouldn't answer any of these questions now, even if I asked.

One more night.

"Are you always like this?" I asked.

His brow furrowed. "What do you mean?"

"With women," I said, looking down. "I mean, I used to know a bunch of guys with your kind of past, and none of them were very... gentle."

He took a deep breath and let it out slowly. "Before I was in prison, things were different."

"But now you're reformed?" I asked, smiling a little.

He gave a wry laugh. "That's the Swedish prison system for you."

He stroked my cheek and traced my eyebrows with his blunt fingertips.

"I guess I see it this way," he said after a moment. "Before I went in this last time, I didn't know anything else. I was a little rougher, and I found women who wanted that, too."

I pulled out the tail of his shirt and slipped my hands onto his bare, hot skin. His muscles twitched under my fingers, and he shifted closer.

"You sure you want to talk about this?" he asked. "Now?"

I nodded.

Jonas frowned a little. "There's nothing soft about being in jail. But there was this librarian who worked there, and everyone lined up for a chance just to sit in the same room with her because she was a woman. She wasn't good looking, but she was kind, like a sister you wanted to keep away from all the bad things in that place. And there she was, every week, sitting at the center of this bad shit we had done. She knew why we were in jail, and she still cared enough to show up. She still saw something worthwhile in us."

He ran his hand through his hair.

"Something about that clicked," he said quietly. "I thought maybe, when I got out, I could meet someone who might see something worthwhile in me."

Worthwhile? I blinked as he spoke these last words.

"I don't have a lot to give," he said, his voice rough. "I've done some bad things that I can't undo. But maybe someday I could love the right person. Maybe even be worthwhile for her."

He wanted someone to love. It was so simple, and with his skin under my fingers, breathing in his scent, I could pretend. For this moment, I could be that person. I leaned against his chest and closed my eyes.

"And you don't think anything like you used to do, anything…" I hesitated. "rougher—you don't think that's what you do with the right person?"

His whole body reacted. When I met his gaze, his eyes flared with unrestrained lust, and his hands tightened around my hips, pressing hard. He stared at me for a long, long time, his eyes on fire. What was he imagining?

He groaned and let go.

"I don't think so," he mumbled, but his eyes still flickered with hope.

"But I'm not the right person."

His eyes blazed hotter. *You* are *the right person*, they said.

No. How could he look at me this way now, like I was everything he had ever wanted? Nothing about this was fair. He was hitting every tender spot I had. Weakening my resolve not to ask for more. I had had enough.

If he was setting the boundaries for what happened after Paris, I was setting the rules for tonight.

I took a deep breath. "Remember back in Stockholm, the very first time when you…?" Now or never. "You held me down. Hard."

Jonas froze, his eyes full of fear. "I'd never do anything you don't want, Alice."

"I know, Jonas," I whispered. "I'm talking about what turned me on."

Jonas worked his jaw, and his eyes were dark and unreadable. The pulse at the base of his neck pounded. "What are you asking for?"

I swallowed hard. "I want to see what happens if I struggle a little."

His breath was quick and harsh. He turned his head away and ran his hand through his hair. "Not a good idea."

"That doesn't turn you on?" I bit my lip. "How did you put it? Sex that feels like fighting."

He shook his head, but his hips rocked into mine, his erection throbbing. Two different answers.

"You're lying," I said.

Jonas bit out a few incomprehensible words.

"I just want to try," I said, my words coming out faster. "Nothing too rough. I can let you know, a safe word or—"

"No." he snapped, his eyes hard. "We're not going anywhere near safe words. If you ever tell me no, we stop. That's not negotiable."

I blinked, my heart galloping faster. "Does that mean you'll try?"

"I don't know."

The noise from the street echoed through the room.

"Maybe just the French phrases from the restaurant?" I whispered.

He groaned, lust burning in his eyes, but he didn't move.

"I want to try this, Jonas. Just once." I paused. "I'd rather it be with you."

Buried in this comment was the kind of manipulation I had sworn I'd never use. The hint that if he turned me down, I'd do it with someone else.

"That's not playing fair, Alice," he bit out. He let out a long sigh of resignation. Then he gave me a hint of a smile, dark and intense. "Fuck, you make me hard."

He grabbed my hand and pressed it against his erection. Slowly, he moved my hand down his long length, pressing harder than I would have on my own. He bent down and whispered, "You sure you want to start this?"

"Yes."

"Then get on your knees," he said, his voice a little colder. "*Suce-moi la bite.*"

He stared at me, unguarded. Raw. Ravenous. This was a glimpse at the other Jonas, the one he kept on a short leash. I got on my knees, my fingers fumbling with his belt. His huge length pressing against his zipper, demanding. Did I trust this side of him, too? My eyes darted up to meet his, and his gaze softened a little. Yes, I did.

I unbuttoned his jeans and carefully lowered the zipper. What a view of him I had gotten earlier in the day. Now I'd get an even closer look.

"Take it out," he said, the coldness back in his voice.

I lowered his boxers over his hips and wrapped my fingers around him. Straining, he thrust into my hand and groaned. He reached for his shirt. Tearing at the buttons, he ripped it off and pulled his t-shirt over his head.

"I want to watch this," he said, his voice heavy with desire. "I want to watch you suck me off."

His word sent a shock of lust through me. Somewhere inside, warning lights went off. I was breaking all my promises to myself. This was the kind of man who would ruin me, make me want everything I couldn't have. But I was too curious, too turned on to stop.

His tip glistened, and I ran my tongue over it.

"That's right," he rasped. "Suck me now."

I angled his erection and took him into my mouth. He let out a long string of foreign words, so I pulled back and did it again. Groans of pleasure filled the room as I explored him with my tongue, my lips. My teeth scraped lightly over his tender skin, and he let out a cry somewhere between pain and ecstasy.

I stopped and met his eyes, fiery and alive. I wanted to see this man unravel. I wanted to make Jonas lose control.

"Keep going," he growled.

He took a handful of my hair and guided me back over him, this time faster. The rumble from deep in his chest pushed me on. I, Alice O'Connor, was going to make this man fall apart.

But he stopped. His grip on my hair loosened, and he muttered something to himself. He pulled out of my mouth, his face twisted in a grimace that bordered on pain.

"You do like that, don't you." It was a statement, not a question, and his voice came out in raspy growls. "You want to bring me to my knees."

I stared up at him. Yes, that's exactly what I wanted. And he wasn't going to give that to me.

He scooped me up and guided me to the bed, positioning me right on the edge. He pushed up my dress and tugged my panties down to my knees.

"You want to know the truth?" he growled. "There are things that get me even harder than your sweet mouth."

One of his hands wrapped firmly around my hips, holding me in place. The other guided his bare erection slowly along my core. Oh, God. I shivered as he moved further and further, circling his tip until my body shook.

"You're so wet," he bit out.

I rocked back, but he held me in place with a dark groan.

Now he was back in control. He continued his slow, seductive torture, pausing at every sensitive spot, teasing until I moaned. I twisted my hips, but he wouldn't let me move. A ripple of pleasure shot through me.

"What do you want, Alice?" He took a couple of harsh breaths. "Because I don't think you're interested in struggling or fighting."

"You're wrong," I whispered. "It turns me on. And I can feel this is turning you on, too." I struggled against his hand to underscore my point.

"Keep going, Jonas," I breathed.

His fingers flexed into my hips, and he thrust, his erection slipping between my legs. "You're going to make me come before we've even started."

He let go of me and walked away, leaving me bent over the bed, my panties around my knees. Was I supposed to just wait like that? I turned around and sat on the bed, stepping out of my panties.

Jonas rummaged through his duffel bag and pulled out a condom. He walked back to the bed and stood in front of me, his erection bobbing just inches away. His hand caressed my cheek.

"What are you looking for, Alice?" he whispered. "I want to clear this up. Because just thinking about you asking some other fucker to make you struggle is taking me to a dark place."

I furrow my brow. "I want to do this with you. Not someone else," I said softly.

He closed his eyes and took a long breath. Then he handed me the condom.

"Put it on," he said, colder again.

His voice sent sparks through me, and my fingers shook as I tore off the wrapper. I played with his hard length a little as I rolled the condom down. He lifted my dress off and dropped it on the ground. I scooted further back on the bed, and Jonas followed, climbing over me.

He settled between my legs. It was the most vanilla of positions, but nothing about him was vanilla. He was raw, volatile, his body taut with tension. Where was this going?

He lowered himself onto his elbows, effectively locking me in place. I tested the restraints of his body, each move sending a delicious erotic rush through me. How could he deny that we both liked a little struggle? Every time I moved, his erection strained against me.

His eyes were stormy and dark. "You know what I think you're looking for?"

My breath caught. He wasn't just talking about bedroom preferences anymore. What was he going to say? Answers rushed through my head, things I couldn't have. Things that didn't belong in this little hotel room.

I closed my eyes. "What am I looking for, Jonas?"

His breaths were soft in my ear. "I think you're running from your past just as hard as I am. I think you're looking for someone to make you stop running."

I stilled. His words were raw, as if he had stolen a glimpse into my private thoughts, thoughts that weren't even fully formed.

"You don't play fair, either," I whispered.

I tugged my hand from his grip and brought it to his face. I moved my fingers along the scar on his jaw, down his corded neck, his heaving muscles, onto his chest until I found the inked bird. It was an ugly black thing, its wing at a painful angle. He closed his eyes as I traced the little design with my fingers. His mouth twisted down.

"You're looking for that, too, Jonas," I whispered.

His jaw worked, but he said nothing. His chest expanded and contracted against mine in heavy breaths, and his pulse ticked at the base of his throat. After long, silent minutes, he kissed me gently and rested his forehead against mine. His erection pressed into my core.

I wove my hand into his hair and brought my lips to his. "So what do we do with that?"

"We fuck," he said, so softly.

I brushed my lips against his once more. "*Baise-moi.*"

Jonas reached between his legs and angled his tip at my entrance. In one hard drive of his hips, he filled me. I gasped. There was nothing on earth that felt this good, this right. His raspy breaths came fast, and his forehead shone with a faint sheen of sweat in the moonlight.

He reach for one of my hands and laced his fingers with mine, pinning it over my head. He had done the same thing earlier today, but this time it was

different. More. He began to move. His muscles rippled with each luscious thrust. His other hand played with my breast, teasing, sending bolts of pleasure through me. I moaned and wrapped my legs around him. His dark blue eyes blazed into mine, intense, full of need.

He wasn't fucking me. He was saying goodbye. To me. To everything we could be if our lives were different. I swallowed the lump in my throat and pulled him down. Our lips met in a hot, explosive kiss. He matched every stroke of my tongue, every bite. I panted, gasping as he came in for more and more. He gripped my hand tighter, and his hips moved faster, harder.

Everything inside exploded in one overwhelming burst. My body trembled as more waves of pleasure washed through me. He chased my pleasure with his own guttural cries, low and desperate, as he took his final strokes.

He groaned, his body heavy on mine, but neither of us moved. I could have stayed there forever. He bowed his head and ran his lips down my earlobe. He kissed my neck and held me tightly. There was nothing left to say, so I kissed him goodbye and pulled him closer.

WARNING

1

MUFFLED VOICES CAME through the wooden conference room door, and I leaned in closer, heart thumping. Was that Jonas's voice? Maybe he wasn't there yet. Or maybe, after three months, I didn't recognize his voice anymore.

No. Impossible. The words he had whispered in Paris still came to me as I lay in bed each night.

You're looking for someone to make you stop running.

His deep, raspy voice still filled my dreams, no matter how much I tried to block it out during the day.

I smoothed back my hair into the neat bun firmly secured at the base of my neck. I had given up on falling back to sleep around five a.m., which left more than enough time to blow my hair perfectly straight. At least one thing was going my way today.

I reached for the door handle, but I couldn't make myself turn it. My heart thumped harder. If I opened this door, I might be face to face with Jonas again. But not the Jonas I knew. The man I had spent two glorious nights with last spring didn't exist. Reading all the details about his past had taken care of that. Every heart-twisting connection I had felt, every spark of hope he had lit was a fantasy, nothing more.

But one thing he had said in Paris rang true. Now that I knew what he had done, I didn't want to see him again. No rational woman would.

I glanced down the empty office hallway. No one was there to witness this moment of weakness. Why couldn't I bring myself to call in sick this morning? Nothing good could come of sitting across the conference room table from him. If Jonas was really as bad as his book suggested, the last glow of my Paris memories would burn out. I deserved those at least, didn't I?

But the bigger danger lay in another possibility. What if I found a trace of the man who had awakened me? What if the irresistible pull of his intense blue eyes drew me in again?

In that case, I was just as messed up as I suspected. Because this man hadn't just served time for theft and armed robbery like my father. He was worse.

It was too late to turn back. I was going to face him for the very last time. Right in front of Neil. Time to pull myself together.

A heavy hand rested on the small of my back. I flinched and whipped around. Neil laughed but didn't take his hand away.

"Scared that monster Jonas Hällström is going to sneak up on you?"

A flush crept up my neck. He had no idea how close he'd come to the truth.

Neil smirked and rubbed his chiseled jaw. "I wonder if he's as fucked up in person as that character in his book. He really went to prison, you know."

I frowned. Yes, I knew.

"But you already met him in Stockholm. Is he here yet?" Neil was standing way too close. Just because we had slept together in the past didn't give him forever rights to look down my shirt. Apparently, he didn't see things that way.

I maneuvered to the side, out of his way. "No idea if he's here."

"The way he beat that guy in a bar until he was almost—"

"We're late, Neil," I said, cutting him off.

Neil straightened his tie and glanced down at my hand, still resting on the door handle. "Then turn the knob."

So I did. I swallowed hard and stepped in. Slowly, I scanned the room. Sanchez. A guy from marketing, sitting next to Neil's red-headed intern, who had somehow arrived before Neil. Why was she here?

And Jonas.

Everything stopped. My traitorous heart leapt in my chest. He wore a white, button-down shirt that covered his tattoos, but nothing could hide the slope of his heavy shoulders or the scars on his knuckles. I forced my gaze up, over his clenched jaw, over the hard, grim line of his full lips, until I reached his eyes. For one brief moment, we were back in Paris. The raw hunger from our last night flickered in his intense gaze. His eyes sparked with deep longing and pain. And then it all disappeared. His expression turned cold. Almost cruel.

Oh, God. I wasn't going to make it through this meeting.

Sanchez stood up as Neil and I entered the room.

"This is Neil Burton from marketing," he said to Jonas.

Jonas's eyes narrowed. I had seen this same expression back in the bar in Stockholm: jaw set, eyes steely. I had seen glimpses of his *don't fuck with me* stare, and now he was giving it to Neil. Jonas crossed the room in a few, purposeful strides, and Neil winced as Jonas's hand closed around his.

"And you remember Alice O'Connor," said Sanchez.

Jonas turned to me. "Of course."

His words came out gruff, and his stare was remote, without any hint of recognition. So why did the sound of his voice echo in currents through my body?

He offered his hand. His eyes stayed cold as his warm fingers enveloped mine. He held on for a little longer than he should have. Heat crept up the base of my neck as I drew in a breath of the same aftershave he had worn last spring.

Shit. Yes, I was just as messed up as I thought.

"Nice to see you again, Ms. O'Connor," said Jonas, but he didn't even try to make it sound convincing.

I blinked, shaking myself out of my daze. "Likewise."

Jonas frowned and let my hand drop. I took a deep breath and headed for an empty chair, heart pounding in overdrive. How the hell was I going to sit across from this man for the next hour?

Last spring, the electric attraction between us started as unprofessional and a little edgy. Now it was wildly inappropriate. Dangerous. Stupid. My twisted heart had to get over it.

Sanchez smiled across the conference table. "Welcome to Boars and Allen, Mr. Hällström."

The red-headed intern lowered the lights, and Sanchez began with an overview of the timeline and marketing ideas. I didn't hear a word he said. My body was on full alert. I twirled my pencil and focused on keeping my face neutral. Jonas didn't glance in my direction or show any sign that he was aware of my presence. At least no one would guess that we had slept together.

I took another quick peek at Jonas. His expression was still hard, but if this Jonas was anything like the man I had known last spring, he was angry.

"It's a great angle," said Neil. "There's a long tradition of literary assholes whose memoirs sell very well, and we think this book fits perfectly into the niche."

"It's not a memoir," snapped Jonas. "Though I'm not denying the asshole part."

"Right, not a memoir," said Neil quickly. "But your own past is similar. You also... well... readers will make the connection, and we can use that."

Jonas's jaw clamped down hard. I stared at him, dying to voice what Neil hadn't had the nerve to say. *You also tried to kill a man.* It was in his book. He had gone to jail for it. What would Jonas do if I looked into his eyes and said those words?

"No. I'm not doing that." Jonas's voice cut in, cold. "I'm not using my own history as a selling point."

"But that's the appeal of this book," said Neil. "Readers love violence and death. Look at your own mystery series. Now you've written about events that come close to your own past, and readers will want the chance to meet a real..."

Neil stopped. The room was dead silent.

Finally, Jonas leaned forward. "Are you going to finish your sentence? A real *what*?" His voice was dead calm.

Neil opened his mouth, but nothing came out.

Sanchez put up his hands. "Just talking ideas, Mr. Hällström. We don't have to go in that direction."

Jonas grunted a response. His hands rested on the table, his scarred fists clenched.

Neil's perky intern cleared her throat. "Here's another idea. Maybe you could write a sequel, where that guy cleans himself up, gets another chance. A redemption story."

Jonas stared at the intern, taking her in for an extra beat. He shook his head. "A guy like that is beyond redemption."

For one, brief moment, his eyes flitted to me. Was he looking for a sign of protest from me? He wasn't going to find it. Or maybe I just imagined the look because the next moment, the hardened version of Jonas was back.

Neil's intern spoke up again. "You could do interviews to put out a softer version of this kind of character. Just something for the readers to connect with."

Jonas's expression didn't ease. "There is no softer version."

The intern's face flushed. Jonas's gaze stayed on the woman, as if fully registering her. I closed my eyes. Another red-haired American woman for him to fixate on. Was he noting her fuller breasts? Her quicker smile? I hadn't missed the comparisons when Neil hired her. Not that it had bothered me. Not until now, when Jonas was sizing up this younger, sexier version of me, too.

I couldn't take one more minute of this.

"I'm sorry. I have another meeting," I lied, standing up abruptly. "But it was nice to see you again, Mr. Hällström. I'll talk to Sanchez about my role from here."

Sanchez's brow furrowed, but he said nothing. I forced a tight smile in Jonas's direction. His eyes darkened a little, but he said nothing.

2

I LOOKED AT my watch. 12:30. Everyone would be at lunch by now. Time to sneak out.

Sanchez had planned to take Jonas somewhere, but I couldn't see Jonas sitting through a business lunch at an upscale Midtown restaurant. Not the Jonas from Paris, and definitely not the guy that sat across from me today.

Head down, I made my way to the elevator. I had to get out of there. What if Jonas walked over to my desk and got my stupid, twisted heart pounding for all the wrong reasons? Again.

Why did I show up today? Even knowing the most awful things about him hadn't stopped my most basic, physical response. That's what it was, wasn't it? Aching want. Maybe I was more like my mother than I thought.

All the more reason to leave the office for the day. And stay away until Jonas was long gone.

I stepped out of the elevator and headed for the glass doors. They slid open, and I stepped out into the cool fall air. I slowed to a stop. Jonas. Only a few steps away. Waiting, leaning against a sign pole. Hands in his pockets, shoulders turned to the cold.

He looked down at his watch. It was my chance to turn around, to slip back inside, but my feet wouldn't move. Slowly, he lifted his gaze. For one, long moment, he just stared at me. His intense blue eyes widened, and he straightened up. I read everything I shouldn't into his gaze—longing, frustration, anger, every emotion I had struggled with these last months. And then there was need. So much need. I sucked in a gasp as a hot spark of desire travelled through me. He parted his lips, the lips I still dreamed about. Then his mouth clamped shut into that grim line I had seen in the conference room.

I glanced around me at the others coming out of the building. No one I recognized. Good. I walked up to Jonas.

"What are you doing here?" I whispered.

Jonas frowned. "I'm waiting for you."

"Why?"

"To say I'm sorry."

I let out a tight laugh. "For what? For trying to kill a man? Because you're apologizing to the wrong person."

He looked at me for a long time. "I didn't mean to let it get so intense between us."

"I can't imagine what happens when you *mean* to get intense," I said dryly. "Oh, wait. I can. Because I've read your book."

He closed his eyes, and his mouth twisted into a deep scowl. His chest rose and fell in a few heavy breaths before he opened them again.

"I'd never let anything like that happen," he said, his voice hard.

"But that's not my point," I snapped.

I glanced over my shoulder and caught sight of the receptionist leaving the building on my lunch break. I gave the woman a tight smile and turned back to Jonas. "Sadly, those days in Paris were some of my best. Ever."

A stormy look crossed his face. "They were some of my best, too, Alice. Nothing changes that."

His words hit me deep inside, throwing me off for a moment. Damn. Why did he have to say something like that right now? I shook my head slowly. Knowing his past changed everything. "Nothing's the same, Jonas."

He looked away. A cab pulled up to the curb. I could jump in it and drive away, just escape. But I didn't. I couldn't. Even knowing that Jonas was capable of far worse than my father wasn't enough to make me run. That was the crux of the problem, wasn't it?

"What the hell did you see in that guy Neil?" Jonas asked. "He's a real asshole."

I raised my eyebrows. "Probably why he likes your book."

"Probably."

I couldn't just stand here on the city street and wait for this to get easier. I still wanted this man, and the urge to breathe in his scent and taste his mouth once more was overwhelming. It was getting worse. The sooner I walked away, the better.

But as I straightened up and drew in a shaky breath, Jonas's eyes darted behind me.

"Shit," he muttered under his breath. "Here we go."

I turned around just as Neil stepped out onto the sidewalk. He tipped his head in our direction. Yes, things were definitely getting worse. But my feet were still firmly planted on the sidewalk.

I had imagined this scene, even fantasized about it back in Paris. Neil was even in a suit on the Sixth Avenue sidewalk, just like I'd imagined. What the hell had I been thinking? That Jonas would come in like some Viking warrior and avenge all past wrongs, making Neil rescind the nasty things he had said to me? Right.

Jonas's mouth was back in that grim line I had seen too many times today, and all the emotion from his eyes was gone. In the conference room Neil hadn't hesitated to poke at Jonas's wounds, knowingly or not. He was probably going to do it again. And next to him, Jonas was scowling, the scar on his jaw an angry red.

Nice taste in men, Alice.

The smart thing to do was to leave. Was this the tenth time the idea had come to me today?

"I thought you were out to lunch with Sanchez," Neil said, giving Jonas a once-over.

Jonas shook his head. "I have something else I need to take care of."

Take care of? Was that me that he needed to "take care of"?

Neil looked at both of us, and his eyes widened. I frowned. Jonas was still standing next to the street sign, but somewhere in our conversation, I had moved closer. Much too close.

"Something to take care of with Alice?" he asked. Then he smiled. "Oh, right. The red-head thing."

Jonas's expression turned dark.

He put his hands up. "Sorry, buddy. Just thought—"

"I'm not your buddy," snapped Jonas. "And where the fuck do you get off talking like that about her?"

Right there, I made a decision. Probably a bad one. Probably one I'd regret. But leaving him right now felt worse.

"Jonas, let's go somewhere else," I said.

He flinched at my voice, his eyes still on Neil. He swallowed and worked his jaw. Then he turned to me. He narrowed his eyes, as if he wasn't sure he trusted my invitation.

"You and Alice?" Neil said incredulously, almost to himself.

But I ignored him, and so did Jonas. His eyes were locked on mine. Finally, he nodded.

Without looking back at Neil, I headed for the taxi waiting at the curb. I climbed in, with Jonas close behind. "Twenty-Second and Third."

The taxi swerved around the corner, and I leaned my head back against the seat. Jonas rested his head in his hands, shaking it slowly. His broad back rose and fell in heavy breaths. The taxi stopped at the light and turned down another street.

Jonas looked at me. "You're going to hear more about this from Neil, aren't you?"

I shrugged. "I doubt Neil will say anything. He's got his own indiscretions."

"I noticed." He sat up and gave me a pointed look. "Let me guess. He hired that intern shortly after you two broke up."

I rolled my eyes. "Yeah. She's cute, isn't she? All that red hair and the peppy smile."

"You don't know what you're talking about," he snapped.

We rode for a few more blocks in silence. Jonas looked out the window at the buildings that rose up on both sides.

"Where are we going?" The crease in his brow deepened. "Your apartment?"

I glared at him. "Hell no."

He flinched but didn't say anything

The taxi pulled up at the corner of Twenty-Second Street and stopped. I paid the driver and climbed out. Jonas followed, keeping a good distance between us.

I nodded to the diner on the corner. "That's where we're going. We'll be left alone."

Alone, but the place was public. I didn't have to say those words aloud. Jonas wouldn't have missed it.

He held the door open for me, and this chivalrous gesture sent a surge of anger through me. I didn't want him to be polite or considerate. I didn't want the other side of him that I had seen in Paris. He wasn't that person.

I headed to my usual spot at the counter. Bad idea. I had sat at this counter listening to other couples' conversations too many times to think we'd get any privacy there.

But I stopped too quickly to head for the booths, and Jonas crashed into me from behind. Rough hands grabbed my shoulders before I stumbled, pulling me back to standing. Against him. Against the hard muscles of his chest. I took a quick breath of the delicious scent of his aftershave. And him. His sharp breaths warmed my neck, echoing deep inside me. Heat rose to my cheeks. Shit, shit, shit.

"Sorry," he muttered, releasing me. He stepped back.

This was a really bad idea.

I didn't look at him. "We'll have more privacy in the back."

The décor of the place had weathered the years well and was now back in retro style. I slid across the light blue vinyl cushion, and Jonas squeezed in across from me. My heart was still on overdrive from our collision, and my cheeks were on fire, my body echoing from his touch. The pulse at the base of his neck ticked fast, but his expression was blank. Neither of us spoke.

The waitress came by with coffee and menus. She took one glance at the grim expression on Jonas's face and left.

"How could you not tell me?" I hissed.

"You didn't want to know." His voice was hard.

"You said assault. But wanting to kill a man? *Trying* to kill a man?" I bit out.

His eyes were cold. "So there are other kinds of assault you'd prefer?"

"No," I snapped.

But the word assault was a lot less vivid than the ten-page description of his attack on that red-haired woman's ex-boyfriend. I'd never forget that scene. The knuckles I had stroked had punched someone until he couldn't stand. The hands that had held me tightly had tightened around someone's neck. The voice that whispered my darkest fantasies was the same voice that had told a man he'd die.

I closed my eyes. "You were only in jail for a few years. I just thought..."

"That I wasn't so bad?" he finished for me. "No. I am that bad. The shorter sentence is because the Swedish system decided I'm reformed."

The last word brought a dark scowl to his face.

I leaned in. "But you don't think so?"

Jonas closed his eyes and said nothing.

The icy anger that had clouded so much of my day melted a little as I studied his expression. Though he had changed his life, he hadn't even begun to forgive himself. However mad I was at him was probably nothing compared to his own self-loathing. He had said something dismissive about redemption stories earlier in the conference room. Did it apply to him, too?

Jonas dropped his head into his hands. His shoulders rose and fell, and he made no effort to defend himself.

"I went to Paris with you," I whispered.

"And now you regret it." Finally, a glimmer of emotion came through in his voice. Anger. And defeat.

I said nothing. I wanted to say yes. I wanted to regret that foolish, impulsive trip to Paris with him. But what made me most angry was the truth: that I still hung onto what we had those few days. That I still wanted what we had between us.

I want to pretend you're my girlfriend for a little longer. He used the word *pretend* in Paris. I just hadn't understood how far from reality our pretend romance had been.

"Alice, I can't take back the things I've done," he said softly.

I looked out the window. "And the other scenes. With the woman. Did you really do those things to her?"

He didn't answer. And the longer he waited, the harder it was to sit across the table from him. He had.

Finally, he looked up at me, and I met his gaze. "I never did anything that she didn't ask for," he whispered. "But I shouldn't have listened to her. I never should have gone so far with her, either." His voice was heavy, like he was much, much older than the man I had met three months ago.

Sex that felt like fighting. He had used those words in Paris, and I had asked for it later that evening. How stupid I had been. I had asked for it, as if it were a sexy game. But it wasn't a game at all to him.

We sat in silence. The waitress came by to take our order, but neither of us had touched our menus. I ordered the first thing that came to mind, a ham and cheese sandwich. Jonas asked for the same, and the waitress left.

"How bad, Jonas?"

He closed his eyes. "Why push this?"

He had a point. Why was I torturing myself? And yet I couldn't leave it. This was my last chance to put together this puzzle, to reconcile the man who had gone to jail with the man from Paris.

We sat in silence.

"Those things you did together in the book," I said. "Are those real?"

He nodded. "Mostly. I changed things that told too much about other people. But whatever you think about that guy – think that about me."

More phrases from Paris flooded back. I made him hungry for things he never thought he could have. What things were those? Rougher things in the bedroom, things that didn't go together with love, as he had put it? Or was he looking for something else?

"Why didn't you tell me?" I asked, a little too loudly. The waitress glanced in our direction. I lowered my voice. "On the last night in the hotel I asked you to—"

"And I said no," he interrupted. "And then you pushed me. You implied you'd do it with someone else."

"And you gave in."

"No," he snapped. A couple two booths away turned to look.

"I didn't give in," he said, quieter, but the anger still seeped through. "I had to choose. Give you just a taste of what you were asking for, or risk that you would find some other sick fuck to do it instead. I don't regret that."

"What if I had pushed you the way your ex-girlfriend did? What if I had told you my ex-boyfriend fucked me harder than you did?"

Jonas looked up at me, surprised and maybe even a little amused. "Neil?"

I huffed out a breath. "You know what I mean."

He massaged his temples.

"I never would hurt you," he said, all traces of amusement gone.

"How do I know that?"

"You don't," he said flatly. "The truth is that I don't trust myself sometimes, Alice. You have no reason to, either. But that statement is as true as anything I've ever said."

The problem was I believed him.

The waitress brought the sandwiches and set them down on the table. A distraction. My stomach turned at the sight of food, but I forced myself to take a few bites, an excuse to look away from Jonas's deep blue eyes. We ate in silence.

He finished his sandwich and moved his plate to the side. He rested his elbow on the table and ran his hand through his hair. "I know that I should wear some kind of warning sign around my neck. That's why I wrote that book in the first place."

His voice cracked with emotion, and he ran his hand through his hair again, leaving a few tufts sticking out in different directions. It was almost sweet. But then I caught sight of his hands. Big, rough hands. No matter how far he ran from his former life, he would always have the hands of a fighter. The top joints of his ring finger bent out at an awkward angle, and white scars cut across his knuckles.

I looked away. It was bad enough that he had a violent past. But what made me want to run the other direction wasn't what he had done. It was how his damaged hands and all the other remainders of his past made him more appealing, not less.

I set down my half-eaten sandwich. "Why are you here, Jonas? I know you had offers from other publishers, offers that were probably better than ours."

He closed his eyes and shook his head.

"I couldn't stop myself," he muttered. "You have every reason to tell me to stay away from you. But I had to see what this would be like, now that you know."

His mouth twisted down. I reached out my hand to touch the deep creases on his forehead. His eyes widened as my fingers brushed against his skin. I froze at the heat radiating from him, then pulled away. I really shouldn't touch him. Just sitting across from him was setting myself up for another months-long Jonas hangover.

How easy would it be to take this man back to my apartment right now? Everything about his past said I should be scared of him. If I could digest the brutality in his book, what else would I come to accept?

My mother probably never thought I'd spend her life pining away for a failed brute of a crook. How many years did it take before my mother realized what her life really was? How many of my father's jail sentences, each longer than the last?

The waitress came by with the check, and Jonas handed a few bills to her before I had a chance to see it.

"Thanks. You didn't have to pay," I said.

His eyes narrowed. He frowned and looked away.

I stood up and headed for the door. It had started to drizzle while we were eating, and the sidewalk was wet. The cold wind blew through my layers, and I hugged my coat tighter around me. I turned the corner and ducked under a little awning. Jonas followed me, his big body blocking the wind. I leaned against the old brick building.

The only thing this lunch had made clear was just how messed up I was over him. Jonas said nothing. He just stood in front of me, waiting.

If I asked him to stay away, he probably would. But I couldn't bring myself to say it.

"What time's your next meeting?" I asked.

He looked at his watch. "Twenty minutes ago. You ready?"

I shook my head. "I'm not going back into the office today."

He frowned. The rain came down harder, blowing drops on his shoulders, but he didn't seem to care.

Finally, he sighed. "So I guess this is goodbye."

Then I was back at our last goodbye in Paris. The kiss on the sidewalk had turned reckless and desperate.

We had said nothing that last time, and there was nothing to say this time, either.

Jonas took a step closer, but he didn't touch me. Aside from the handshake at the office and the collision in the diner, he hadn't touched me at all. Was staying away just as hard for him as it was for me? One look at his face told me it was worse. His mouth hovered so close, and his breaths warmed me.

"Once more?" His voice came out rough.

Just one more kiss. We had come this far. Could I deny myself one last chance to taste his soft, warm lips? Just one more chance to rest my hands on the hard planes of his chest? Just one more time had gotten me into this mess in the first place, but now, faced with the decision again, I couldn't turn it down.

"Yes," I whispered.

Jonas didn't react right away. He leaned one arm against the building at my back and fixed his intense gaze on me. There was nowhere else to look but into the stormy blue eyes I had tried so hard to forget. I hadn't forgotten at all. That was the problem.

Slowly, he raised his hand to my cheek. His thumb caressed my lips, giving me all the time in the world to back away. But I was long past backing away.

I closed my eyes, and his lips brushed against mine. A groan rose from deep inside his chest, and I answered it with my own desperate sounds. Everything about him felt so raw. So good. He came in for another kiss. His lips stroked mine, coaxing them open for him.

As I lost myself in the heady relief of finally touching him, the tone shifted. His hand slipped behind my neck, and his tongue persuaded, begged until I met his every stroke with more and more hunger. I fumbled with his open coat. Just a little closer, a little more. His muscles flexed under my touch. I would never get enough of this man. I gasped for breath and went back for more, caressing his tongue with mine. But all too soon, he slowed me down. He pulled back and kissed my neck. His eyes met mine for a long, hot look, and then he pulled me in again, holding me tight.

"Why do you have to be so good at that?" I whispered.

He let me go and straightened up. God, he was big. I had forgotten how it felt to be so close to him, to a man whose presence could be used both as a threat and as a promise.

He shoved his hands into his pockets. "I'm staying at the Hilton on Fifty-Fourth and Sixth. I'm leaving tomorrow."

Jonas didn't wait for my response. He turned into the gusts of rain and walked away.

3

ONCE I HAD read somewhere that the brain makes a decision long before the conscious mind registers it. Which meant that though I may spend minutes or hours or, in this case, an entire afternoon making a decision, much of the time was wasted. My brain had sealed the deal long before I thought I chose.

As my taxi headed uptown, I searched for the moment when the scales truly tipped. Surely it wasn't a half hour ago, when I finally changed out of my sweatpants and slipped on a dress. Was it when I picked up Jonas's manuscript once more and re-read all the most brutal parts, registering each gut-punch of disgust, and, even worse, each stir of longing for the man tormented by this past? Or was it when I sat down on my bed and opened the little box of photos from my childhood, back when my father was still around? Likely neither of those.

My brain had probably locked in on an answer hours before that, back on the rainy street, just around the corner from my apartment. In fact, I could probably pinpoint the exact moment my fate was sealed: when Jonas's warm lips brushed against mine. It had quickly spiraled from goodbye into want and need, but for that first moment, his lips said something else.

I'm giving myself to you.

Which was ridiculous. Even if I had read him right, I knew better than to believe it. Men made promises all the time, promises they meant to keep. But far away from the bedroom, promises didn't hold. No one thought with their heart all the time. Not Jonas, not anyone.

The rain had stopped somewhere in the afternoon, but the streets were still slick. The sun's reflection flashed off the windows of the buildings I passed.

Could Jonas's past ever really fade, or would it always be present? His book described organized fighting, evenly matched, fully consensual. And the bar fights, provoked, unevenly matched. And the man Jonas had meant to kill.

The Swedish prison system released him, but what did it mean to be reformed? A prison sentence was meant to be a punishment that ended when he walked out, not a branding that lasted forever. But how many people got out of that life after one sentence? My father never stayed out of trouble for long.

But that kiss. That kiss on the sidewalk was an all-too-vivid reminder of everything I had let myself want in Paris. It didn't match the man in his book. The man who would let the dark games with his ex-girlfriend get so far out of hand.

The taxi pulled into the hotel's circular entrance. I paid the driver and climbed out. I stared at the glass doors in front of me. Even if I knew his room number, I wasn't going up there. Hotel rooms meant only one thing. Was I there to spend another night with Jonas, knowing his past?

Maybe my brain had already decided that, too. The answer couldn't be yes, could it?

I took a step and then another, and the doors parted. I walked into the enormous lobby and stopped a few feet in. Not what I expected. I had imagined something more dimly lit, maybe with an intimate little restaurant off to the side where I could gather myself together. Instead the hotel lobby was an open circular room with enormous columns and a large statue in the middle. One side was lined with desks, and the other opened up to hallways. I stood in the doorway as guests jostled their luggage around me.

"Can I help you?" A man in the hotel's uniform walked toward me.

I blinked. This was a mistake. I shouldn't have come.

"No, thanks," I said to the man and turned around.

And there, in front of me on the drive, Jonas walked up the sidewalk. He didn't see me at first. When he looked up, his eyes widened, as if I were the last person he had expected to see. His movements slowed until, finally, he stopped a few feet away from me.

"Hi," I said softly.

He raised his eyebrows. "You're here." He didn't look so thrilled to see me. More stunned than anything else.

I crossed my arms. "I'm not sure what I'm doing here."

He didn't react. The guests walked in and out of the hotel, passing us on both sides. One woman slowed as she walked by Jonas, sizing him up appreciatively. Would she give him that same look if she knew he had been to prison?

Finally, Jonas's expression softened. He reached up and rested his hand on my cheek. The gesture was meant to be tender, but the scrape of his large fingers on my skin sent a wave of longing through me. His eyes flared with heat, and for a moment I thought he might kiss me.

But he dropped his hand and frowned. "I need to grab something from my room. If you're still around when I get back, we can both try to figure out what we're doing here."

A FEW MINUTES later, Jonas appeared from the elevator hallway. He had changed out of his business shirt into jeans and a zip-up hoodie. My heart quickened. He didn't see me. He slowed as he entered the lobby, coming to a stop not far from me. He looked around, frowning. His heavy shoulders rose and fell.

What would he do if he thought I'd left? I had been in his shoes back in Paris, when he didn't show up at the airport. But when I caught a glimpse of the defeated look on his face, I couldn't hang back any longer.

"Jonas?"

He turned to me, and his face opened in a slow smile. He crossed his arms over his chest, emphasizing the size of his biceps, even through his sweatshirt. It was impossible to ignore his overwhelming physicality. There was so much of him to take in.

"You're still here."

I nodded.

"You hungry?" he asked.

I shook my head. "Not yet. You?"

"No."

"Where should we go?" I asked.

He shrugged. "Doesn't matter."

"You're in New York," I laughed. "Don't you want to see something? The Empire State Building? The Statue of Liberty?"

He smiled a little but shook his head. "How about Central Park?"

I glanced at my watch. "We probably have another hour before the sun goes down."

He furrowed his brow in confusion.

Oh, right. While I'd never walk alone at dusk in Central Park, Jonas lived a different life. In fact, he'd be the type of guy I'd cross the street to avoid at night. What would it feel like to have a boyfriend like Jonas, to walk out on the dark New York streets, knowing he could take just about anything that came? Tonight I'd get a taste.

"I know a good place," I said. "Let's get a cab."

He followed me to the street and opened the door of the taxi for me. I gave the driver directions and stole a glance at Jonas. The scar along his hard jaw and the day's worth of stubble made him look even grittier when he wasn't smiling. And he wasn't anymore.

He was staring at me.

"No curly hair today?" he asked.

I wrinkled my nose. "When I let it stay curly, it gets too wild. Especially in the rain."

Jonas fingered a stray lock of hair that had escaped from the bun but didn't say anything.

"You didn't think I'd come?" I asked softly.

He shook his head warily. "I'm glad you did, but I'm not sure where this is going." He looked over at me, his mouth pulled into a wry smile. "Things work better when I know what's coming."

Of course. The man in his book was all action and reaction, guided by anger, lust and the drive to stay on top. The man sitting next to me kept those parts of himself on a short leash. How much did he struggle every day to keep these parts of him under control? I had seen hints of this side of him in Paris, but today in the conference room, I understood why he spent his days alone, shut off from the rest of the world. He shaped his new, reformed life around the idea that he wasn't fit for everyday company, no matter what his release papers said.

But who was I to judge? I held my own life under just as tight control. I arrived at work early and left late, making sure I'd never be out of a job. That I'd never have to rely on someone else. Jonas had been right in Paris. Every choice I made was measured on a scale of whether or not it would take me farther from my past.

Every decision except the ones that involved Jonas.

We drove along the edge of the park, lined with the lush colors of fall. It had been years since I had been to Central Park, back when I still lived in Brooklyn. Back when the course of my life wasn't as set.

THERE WAS WARINESS in the way Jonas kept his distance, hands in his pockets, as he walked into the park. The oranges and yellows of fall had taken over, drowning out the lush green of summer. The trees and the grass sparkled with the sheen of water from the rain, and the air was still wet and heavy. I hugged my coat closer against the cold.

"Central Park is bigger than I thought it would be," said Jonas. "I've heard everything in this country is big, but it's still surprising."

I nodded. "I haven't seen most of it. Just the Met
– the museum we passed – and this place I'm taking you.
But there's a lot of other things I've always meant to do.
A zoo, concerts in the summer, an ice rink in the winter."

He tilted his head at me. "Do you skate?"

"Not at all. You?"

Jonas smiled. "They start us Swedes on skates in
preschool, if you can believe it."

I couldn't even begin to imagine Jonas as a child.

"Did you ever play hockey?" I asked.

"Sure."

"I bet you were good at it." I could see him on
the hockey rink, a little older, towering over the other
guys. Though if his past was any indication, he probably
would have spent most of the time in the penalty box.

Jonas sighed. "I tried playing for a while, but
team sports aren't really my thing. And I didn't get along
with the coach. Besides, it costs a lot of money to play."

"And your parents couldn't pay for it?"

Jonas shrugged. "I never asked."

He had mentioned the lack of money before.
How hard did he have to struggle to get what he wanted?
If he was anything like me, he probably squashed
hundreds of dreams, knowing there was no use pining
after something so far out of reach.

"Do you ever wonder how your life might have
gone differently?"

He frowned and rubbed the back of his neck. "I
used to think about that all the time when I was a

teenager. How would it feel if I lived in a nice house instead of a shitty, run-down apartment? What was it like to have a father who could hold down a job and didn't spend his welfare money on beer? But what's the point of thinking about the things you can't have?"

I nodded. Jonas had never said a word about his family before. We walked along the sidewalk, dodging puddles, and I waited to see if he'd add anything else.

"But lately, I've wondered about what would have happened if I had applied to college," he said after a while. "I had the grades, and college is free in Sweden, so I could have gone. But I just couldn't see myself in that life." He glanced over at me and added, "You know, college, a job in an office with a boss, married, kids, all that shit."

"All that shit," I echoed, smiling a little.

He smiled too. "But maybe there were more than just two options."

Back in high school, I only knew about a couple choices, too. I had taken pains to avoid the pregnant option, so I was left with finding a way out of my neighborhood, into a life that didn't involve words like eviction notice, repeat felon and parole. Everything I swore I'd never face again.

Or so I had thought. Jonas was shaking up these pillars in my life.

The park was far from empty, despite the fading glow of the sun behind the trees. The sidewalk was filled with joggers, people walking their dogs and a few couples.

I pointed to a lookout spot with stone steps down on either side. "This is what I had in mind."

I walked over to the carved railing that overlooked the fountain and the lake, and Jonas followed close behind. He rested his hands on the stone and looked out at the bucolic scene, so removed from city life. The oranges of the fall leaves reflected off the water, shimmering in the fading light. It had been so long since I had stood here. It was almost as if I had been another person back then. And now I was here with Jonas.

He was silent. He turned around and rested against the heavy stone railing, his eyes on me.

"This is unexpected," he said, eyebrows raised. "I thought you weren't into mushy romantic stuff."

He was smiling, but his deep blue eyes searched mine.

"I'm not," I said. "I've only been here once, a long time ago."

He gave me a quizzical look. "If I lived in a city like this, I'd come here every day."

I shrugged.

"Let's go down by the water," I said.

We walked down the flights of stone steps, onto the terrace. The fountain wasn't running, and beyond it the lake was still and quiet. At one end, the Boathouse patio glowed softly in the setting sun, the silhouettes of patrons in the windows.

Jonas's warm breath teased my neck. He was close, so close. If I turned my head, I could run my fingers along the stubble of his jaw, guiding his full lips to mine. It was happening again, that flare of attraction that grew hotter each time I came near him. I wanted to touch him, to go back to that easy comfort of Paris. Just for one more night?

I straightened up. "Let's walk."

I headed for the path along the shore, and Jonas followed. The silence grew heavier as the memories I had pushed away all flooded back. The lines of his tattoos. The hard muscles of his chest under my fingers. The weight of his heavy body on mine. And the words he spoke.

No. I couldn't go over those words again, not now. I searched for a safe topic, but nothing came.

"Are those row boats for rent?" asked Jonas, pointing further along the shore.

I nodded. "Probably too late to go out today."

A gust of wind blew leaves across the path.

"Have you ever done that?" he asked.

I nodded slowly. "Once."

"With Neil?"

I snorted. "Not a chance." I chuckled at the image of Neil in his expensive suit, climbing into a boat. "Not his thing."

"Then who was it?"

"A guy from high school." Shit. Maybe I could steer this conversation in another direction. Or maybe

158

he'd know to drop it, the way he had back in Paris. Except this wasn't Paris, not even close.

"A boyfriend?"

I shrugged. "Not really." I glanced up at him.

He was staring at me, his eyes filled with challenge. "You know every fucking mistake I've made. And you're not going to tell me about this?"

I huffed out a breath. "Fine. I was sixteen, and he was two years older. I didn't think he had ever given me a second glance, so I couldn't believe it when he asked me out. We took a cab here from Brooklyn, which costs a ton, and then he took me out on one of these boats. And the whole time I couldn't get over that he had asked me out."

I swallowed, keeping my voice even. "We walked around a little, and he bought me ice cream. It was the kind of thing I never thought would happen to me." I took a deep breath. "Then we went back to his place, and he wanted me to suck him off."

Jonas stopped. I turned around, and his face had that eerie, expressionless look I had seen earlier. "Did you?"

I frowned. "Well, no. But for a little while I thought he might force me to."

Jonas didn't move.

There was no reason to hold back at this point, so I added the last humiliating details. "It turned out that another guy had bet him that he couldn't get me to suck him off. So I told him I wouldn't, but he could say

159

whatever he wanted. I wouldn't deny it. I guess that was what he really wanted."

Jonas closed his eyes. The pulse pounded at the base of his throat. When he looked at me again, there was pain in his intense gaze. He took a tentative step toward me and slowly put his arms around me. When I didn't pull away, he brought me closer, tucking me against his broad chest.

"Why the fuck did you ask me for those things in Paris?" His harsh, angry tone contrasted with the slow, soothing strokes of his hand down my back.

I let out a shaky breath and let myself relax against his chest. There was no good answer except that I was curious. Back in high school, it was the same. I had known what that guy's reputation was, and I still went out with him. I blamed it on my parents, my neighborhood and all the other things in my life that let the biggest guy that oozed violence and virility rise to the top. But this time, with Jonas, I was too old to blame anyone but myself.

Jonas's chest expanded and contracted, and his breath was warm in my hair. His arms moved to my shoulders, and he pulled away, holding me at a distance.

"What the hell were you thinking?" he said softly. "I could have…" He shuddered. "You shouldn't have put that kind of trust in me."

I hugged my coat closer and looked away. A woman passed with a tiny dog, eyes averted, sticking close to the side of the path. New Yorkers don't stare, not even if they pass a *don't fuck with me* guy glaring down at a woman on a darkening path.

Jonas shifted on his feet, waiting for me to speak. When I didn't, he stepped closer, towering over me. As if I needed another reminder about just how big he was. A bolt of white-hot lust ran through me. Oh, God. It was like I was hard-wired to respond to him when he was all worked up. And he knew it.

"Why are you here?" he asked, his voice lower. "If you want one more night of taking our clothes off together, I won't say no. But I need to know that now, before we go any further."

His words set off another rush of desire, and my breath hitched. If I couldn't decide what I wanted after an afternoon of restless pacing in my apartment, I certainly wasn't going to make any revelations when every muscle in my body was begging to touch him.

Jonas seemed to register this shift into more sexual territory. His eyes narrowed.

"Is that why you're here?" he asked, his voice hard. "For another night? Because you've decided I'm not too dangerous to fuck one more time?"

This was no longer a question. It was an accusation. I glanced down the path, but no one was around. The sun had set, and the park was getting dark.

"Fuck you, Jonas," I whispered. "You're the one who set the limits when we left Paris."

He scowled but said nothing. All the frustration from the afternoon was bubbling up, and I couldn't stop it from spilling out.

"No, Jonas. My problem is that you don't scare me," I said. "My problem is that despite all the awful things you've done, I still came to your hotel. That I want you even more now that I know more about you. That's what scares me."

I took a couple deep breaths. My heart was racing, but I didn't look away from his eyes as he glared down at me. He took a step and then another, forcing me to back up until I was against one of the trees on the edge of the path.

"Does it scare you that I know you live around the corner from where we ate lunch today?" he asked, his voice hard. That got my attention. My apartment? The one place in the world that was my own? But Jonas didn't give me time to think further. "Does it scare you that I'd know how to break into your apartment whenever I wanted?" He leaned in closer. "You read my book. You know what I've done."

If this were a scene from a movie, I would have rolled my eyes. No sane woman would wander on a dimly lit footpath in Central Park with an ex-con with a penchant for violence. But I was that moth right now, my traitorous body about to burst into flames. And still I didn't back down.

"That guy back in high school who took me out on the boat could break into my apartment – he and every one of his friends," I snapped. "But my front door is still standing. There's a difference between what you're capable of and what you choose to do."

His hands were suddenly under my ass, and he pressed my core against his rock-hard erection. He groaned. "Does it scare you that I get hard when you're angry with me?" he whispered. "That I've already imagined all the crudest ways I could win this argument?"

I let out a little moan. If he was trying to scare me away, trying to show that he was just as much of an asshole as every other guy like him, it wasn't having the effect he intended. Or maybe it was. I was so close to the edge. There was nothing left to do but throw myself off.

"Then do it," I said. "Show me what I should be scared of."

Jonas growled, actually growled. His mouth crashed onto mine, his teeth against mine, his tongue plundering my mouth. It was crude, full of lust without finesse, without restraint. Finally, he wasn't holding back. I tried to match his strokes, but he bombarded me with his hungry mouth, with his rough hands and the power of his body. His fingers pressed hard into my ass as he thrust into me. I squirmed against his hold and got nowhere. And, damn it, it was heaven.

He broke off the kiss. His savage gaze glowed in the faint light.

"You don't know what you're asking for," he spat out.

I glared at him. "Do you know how condescending you sound?"

He pressed his lips into the base of my neck and sucked hard. I yelped in surprise. He moved his mouth a little lower, into the tender hollow above my collar bone. I closed my eyes and tipped back my head. He sucked again, this time harder, and a tremor ran through his body, pressed against mine. His groan was loud, unrestrained. His eyes met mine, filled with bottomless hunger, aching with insatiable need.

"I won't stop until I've gone too far," he whispered. "Does that scare you?"

Before I could register his words, his mouth descended on mine again, greedy, taking more and more. His body pressed my back against the tree trunk, and his hands slipped under my coat, searching for my breasts. His palms were hot, even through the material of my dress. I closed my eyes and leaned my head back against the rough bark of the tree. He found my nipples and squeezed, thrusting his rock-hard length against me at the same time. A loud cry escaped from my mouth, startling me. We were so far past public decency.

I opened my eyes and froze. Only a few feet away was a guy, not much smaller than Jonas, gaping at us.

"Oh," I gasped, straightening up.

Jonas stopped, his whole body tense. His eyes went to mine and then followed my gaze to the man. In an instant, everything about Jonas changed. His arms rose around me in a cocoon, one hand cradling my head.

"Stay the fuck away from us," Jonas growled, his eyes fixed on the man.

The stranger didn't move. He looked from Jonas to me, then back to Jonas. Did the guy think I was in danger? Jonas clearly wasn't getting a good read on the situation. Or maybe I wasn't.

"It's okay, Jonas," I whispered.

He shook his head a little.

I turned to the man. "I'm fine. We're…" I searched for the right words. "We're together."

The guy frowned. "Then get a room."

"Good point," Jonas muttered. Finally, his arms loosened a little.

The man scowled, his eyes darting between us, and walked away. I took a few more gulps of air, trying to slow down my breaths.

Jonas's arms loosened further, and he backed away a little. He glanced around, as if he were taking in our surroundings for the first time.

"We need to get out of here," he said quietly.

I nodded, and he adjusted what must have been the world's most uncomfortable erection. I straightened out my dress, and we started back along the footpath, toward the Boathouse. He didn't touch me, though he walked much closer than before, looking around.

I was restless and edgy. All along, I had been bracing myself for an undercurrent of violence, waiting for its ugly head to finally rear. But even tonight, when I made myself most vulnerable and challenged him to give me his worst, he had come to me with something different. It was hunger, a hunger that needed more than just physical satisfaction.

I'm won't stop until I've gone too far.

The words he had whispered were about something much different than violence. Something much more intimate. I was beginning to suspect that I had him all wrong.

I glanced up at Jonas. Deep creases lined his forehead, and his jaw was clenched. He hadn't even looked in my direction since we started walking.

He was retreating back into his thoughts, and by the look on his face, none of them were good. The lights from the Boathouse glowed in the evening. Inside, couples were eating dinner, talking, doing the things normal couples did. I frowned. If we walked into that restaurant right now, the stormy look on Jonas's face would silence conversations. Even if Jonas and I found our way past one more night, would we ever be one of those regular couples?

We slowed our pace, both staring into the windows taking in the romantic scene. Jonas's forehead was lined with deep creases.

"You're not disgusted with me?"

"No," I said softly. Not at all.

"Not afraid?"

I never felt physically threatened by him, if that's what he was asking. But there was more to be afraid of than brute physical violence.

I sighed. "Not in that way."

Most of the evening light had faded.

"What do we do now?" I asked, raising an eyebrow at him. "Go up to your room?"

I meant it as a joke, but he didn't smile.

"No," he said. "I'm not interested in another night in a hotel room with you."

He was turning me down? The physical connection was our one certainty. And he was rejecting it? He had, in fact, steered us away from his hotel as soon as I arrived.

My face flushed, and I looked away. I had spent all afternoon agonizing over a decision that he had already made for us.

Jonas cupped my cheek, gently guiding my gaze back to him. "I'm done with hotel rooms. I want to go back to your apartment and order bad take-out food and talk and kiss and talk some more."

I froze. My apartment? No.

"I don't think so," I said.

He scowled. "So you're willing to have sex with me in a hotel room, but I'm not allowed in your apartment?"

I shook my head. "You don't understand. My apartment is..." I frowned. "It's not just you, Jonas. No one comes to my apartment."

It wasn't exactly a rule. It had just worked out that way. I met people out, for dinner or over coffee. My apartment was too tiny and out of the way for anyone to visit. My mother had never even made the trip there. And now Jonas wanted to come?

His eyes were narrowed, and he worked his jaw. "We've done this all before," he said, gesturing to the park. "Walk around until I get too hard to think straight, then go fuck. I don't care how much I want you. That's not what I'm here for."

I frowned. "Couldn't we just go to a bar or something?"

"And what happens after that?" His fingers glided over my shoulder, stroking my arm. "Because I don't want to spend another couple hours listening to your voice, touching you, breathing in the scent of you, and then cut it all off again."

I huffed out a breath. "And this is all about what you want?"

He closed his eyes. "No. I'm just being upfront. I want to go back to your apartment and sit on your couch with you. I want to peek at your photos and your bookshelf when you're not looking. I want to undress you on your own bed, not in another hotel room."

More if his words from Paris came back to me. *I want everything a selfish prick in jail can't have.*

"I want more, Alice," he said, raising his voice. "I'm a messed up asshole with a record. You have every reason to run the other direction as fast as you can. But I'm here on that slim chance that you're not going to run. That you feel the same connection that I do."

I stared at him, trying to register his statement. I had lost myself in this fantasy back in Paris. That this could be something more. But it wasn't real. We had only spent a few days together. And even if I listened to my body, screaming that these things didn't matter, he still was offering everything on his terms.

"What do you mean by more?" I crossed my arms. "You come to my apartment and you look at my photos and browse my bookshelves and lie in my bed. And then you leave tomorrow. Is that more?"

His large hands cupped my cheeks, and he pressed his lips against mine, letting them linger, our breaths mingling. "I don't know."

At the beginning of the day, I had told myself I couldn't face this man again. Now, I was considering bringing him back to my apartment. *My apartment.*

He ran his hand through his hair and frowned. Then he dug into the front pocket of his jeans and pulled something out. Something small.

"I've been waiting for a good time to do this," he mumbled, "but it looks like there isn't going to be one."

He opened his hand a little and held out his palm. In it was a rectangular box, all black with white script. In French. My heart jumped.

"For you," he said softly.

My heart squeezed painfully. I took the little box and pulled off the lid. Nestled inside were a pair of earrings, made of long, wispy strands of silver. The ones I had eyed in the Paris window. Beautiful, more elegant than any of the other jewelry I owned. He had bought them for me.

"I should have gotten them the first time, when we were standing there," he said.

I blinked up at him. "You went back?"

He nodded. "A couple weeks ago. They were still in the window."

I fingered the delicate silver strands but didn't take them out.

"But you thought I wouldn't want anything to do with you anymore," I whispered.

Jonas closed his eyes and sighed. "You had every right not to. But I couldn't stop thinking about it. About how much I wanted to see you again. And once I get my mind set on something, I can't let it go."

I stared at the earrings. Never once when I stood in that Paris window did I imagine I'd actually own them.

"What would you have done with them if I hadn't shown up tonight?"

He shrugged his heavy shoulders. "Keep them. Remind myself that there can be a little light in this dark world."

Tears pricked at the corners of my eyes.

"This hurts," I said, gesturing to him, the quiet lake, and the dreamy glow of the Boathouse. "I don't even know why."

The corners of his mouth turned down. "All of it hurts, Alice. The last three months have hurt. Let's make it worth it."

The fall leaves skidded across the sidewalk, and the din of the city streets found its way through the trees. I put a hand on my hip. "We don't even know each other. This is just fantasy and lust. It won't last."

"Maybe." He nodded slowly, his dark blue eyes fixed on me.

I had expected him to put up more of a fight, but he didn't. Did he understand how unrealistic it was to want more? And he still came?

I shook my head. "We're not seeing each other clearly. We're just projecting all our hopes onto each other."

He reached out to tuck a strand of hair behind my ear. He ran his fingers down my neck, sending a shiver through my body. "What are those hopes?"

"I don't know." I squeezed my eyes shut as his touch echoed through my body. It was getting harder and harder to back away.

His hand rested on my neck, his thumb gently stoking, coaxing. "Don't you want to find out?"

I almost said no. But when I lifted my gaze to his stormy eyes, the deep surge of warmth was too much to resist. Did I dare to hope for everything, just once?

I swallowed hard and let out a shaky breath. "Okay. Let's go to my apartment."

He groaned out a few words, probably in Swedish. Then he came closer, his lips almost touching mine.

"This, right now," he whispered. "This is more than I could hope for."

He found my hand, shoved in my jacket pocket, and brought it to the warmth of his neck. His pulse beat furiously under my fingers. "My heart feels like it's going to explode."

He brushed his lips against mine, closing the last distance between us. The slow press of his mouth was unbearably tender. How could this be the same man who had kissed me with all the crude lust of a man just out of prison? He coaxed my mouth with luscious strokes of his full lips against mine. The kiss was gentle, full of heartache and deep longing.

It was as if he spoke a secret language, one I never realized I knew, one that got under my skin and went straight to my aching heart. I and Jonas were stepping off a cliff, falling into the darkness.

Jonas broke off the kiss and sighed. He reached for my hand and looked around at the winding paths of the park. "How the hell do we get out of this place?"

4

WE HEADED TO Seventy-Second Street and found a cab. I climbed in and gave the driver directions, and Jonas pulled me against his large body. He wrapped his arms around me, and I closed my eyes, breathing in his scent, concentrating on the steady rise and fall of his chest.

Neither of us spoke. Something between us had shifted, and we had found ourselves in a new place together, too fresh and raw to disturb. But it was real. The man from Paris – the man he claimed didn't exist – was next to me again. Or some version of him.

The driver dropped us off in front of my building, and the car disappeared down the dark street. I pointed up at the old brick building with its black metal fire escape and dimly lit windows.

"This is it," I said and started for the door.

But Jonas didn't follow me.

"You come home alone to this place every night?"

I turned around. He was still at the curb, looking up and down the empty sidewalk. His expression was hard, almost angry, and his voice was deceptively calm.

I sighed. "Yes, but it's usually light. Or I have the driver wait until I get into the building."

He frowned but didn't say anything.

"Come on," I said, motioning up the stairs. "You wanted to see my apartment, didn't you?"

His expression softened a little, and he rubbed the back of his neck. Finally he nodded and followed me up the steps.

We walked through the narrow hall, his large body alert, ready for whatever came. For once, I didn't grab my pepper spray as I rounded the steps to my apartment. The light by my door was burnt out, and I fumbled with my keys. I glanced up at Jonas, and he looked from the burnt-out bulb back to me. He didn't have to say a word. I knew what he was thinking.

"I can take care of myself, you know," I said. "I've lived in New York all my life."

Jonas shook his head. "There are a lot of sick fucks out there. I've met them." He gestured to the dark bulb and the narrow staircase that blocked a clear view of the hall. "I don't like this."

I stopped fumbling with my keys and turned to face him. "What the hell, Jonas? Are you here to tell me why it's not safe to be on my own? That I need someone to take care of me? Because I've already heard it."

I gritted my teeth. Fuck him for making me wonder what it would feel like to live with a man like Jonas, to not be on constant alert every time I left my apartment. Fuck him for making me want to let down my guard, just for a little while. Because he wasn't going to live here. He wasn't going to take care of me. We'd never come home together like this after a quiet dinner date. Even if we both wanted those things, the government probably didn't give work visas to ex-cons. It was a miracle that we even let him into the country at all.

Jonas closed his eyes and ran his hand through his hair.

"Sorry," he muttered. He glanced at me, his deep blue eyes wary. "I don't know how to do this."

I blinked up at him, and for a moment he looked lost.

"Let's go in," I said.

I turned the key, and we walked inside. The hallway was usually just big enough to take off my coat, but with Jonas there, we were up against each other. I raised my eyebrows. "It's a little tight."

"I don't mind," he said. He slipped off his shoes and maneuvered around me, his large hands resting on my hips as he shuffled by. He paused, his breath in my hair, before he moved out of the hallway.

I hung up his sweatshirt, and he wandered into my apartment. My pulse kicked up. The place was tiny, and the only thing younger than me about the space was the coat of paint I had given the walls when I moved in. The linoleum on the kitchen counters was yellowing, and one of the windows had jammed shut long before I arrived.

But Jonas didn't seem to notice any of those details. He was looking at my things.

The problem with having a guest in a studio apartment was the bed. The narrow twin mattress was pushed into the corner, with a pile of pillows right underneath the windows. The fact that I had a bed was no secret, but when Jonas's gaze went straight for it, my heart jumped. There was no subtlety in inviting a man straight to my bedroom.

Jonas shoved his hands into his pockets and wandered into the room. He was wearing a t-shirt that did nothing to hide the thick muscles that flexed with every move. I leaned against the doorway, watching him as he invaded my space with his big, irresistible body. He followed the long, low bookshelf along the brick wall, stopping occasionally for a closer look at a title. He pulled out a mystery by another Swedish writer and turned back to me.

"Per Henrik Högberg," he said, holding up the book. "He's pretty good."

I nodded. The heat must be on overdrive today. Either that, or I just couldn't get past having Jonas in my place. Whatever it was, I was getting antsy. I walked across the room to crack the working window, and the noises of the street rushed in.

"I'm impressed," he said. "You weren't expecting me to come over, and your bed is made."

I shrugged. "Habit, I guess. My mother put me in charge of cleaning from a young age."

"Looks great. I bet the bathroom is even clean."

I laughed. Actually, it was. What else was I supposed to do when I woke up at five this morning?

Jonas smiled. "If you ever stop in to my place for a surprise visit, the bathroom definitely won't be clean."

A surprise visit to Stockholm? He knew I didn't have money for that kind of thing. What kind of future was he imagining?

He continued down the bookshelf, coming closer and closer. But he wasn't looking at me. He was looking at the little photo perched where the books ended. A shot of my mother and me at Coney Island from so many years ago. He had coaxed his way into my own, private space, and now he had found the only photo I kept out in my apartment. Jonas was so quiet, so still now. And I was about to burst.

He picked up the frame and held it in the light. I braced myself for the questions that were bound to come, but he set the photo down without saying a word. Maybe he wouldn't ask. My shoulders sagged with relief. This was already way too much.

But then he turned to me, his blue eyes stormy. "What happened with your father, Alice?"

"My father?" I frowned. Why did he want to talk about this?

But Jonas's gaze didn't waver. "I want to know."

"There's not a lot to tell," I said. "He was third rate in every way possible. As a father, as a husband, as a thief and a thug."

"But your mother took him back," he said softly.

I sighed. "Every time."

"Was he ever violent?"

I winced. "Not with me."

He lifted his hand to my cheek, caressing with a softness a man like him shouldn't be capable of. And he waited.

I sighed. "I'm not sure about my mother. There were times I wondered, when I thought I heard—"

No. I couldn't say it. I had closed that door, and I wasn't going back there. Not even for Jonas.

His eyes flashed with anger. He waited. But there was nothing left to say.

He furrowed his brow. "And you're worried you'll end up like your mother?"

I shook my head. "No. I'll never let myself end up there."

If it meant that I was lonely for the rest of my life, so be it. I had told myself this hundreds of times over the years. But it wasn't until I left Paris that I understood just how lonely the rest of my life could be.

He slipped his other arm around my shoulder and shifted closer. I stiffened, a little startled. For once, I wasn't sure I wanted him so close, but he didn't pull away. I took a shaky breath, and he stroked my side with his thumb. The deep creases on his forehead were still there, and his eyes were vulnerable, full of regret.

"I told you before that I would never do anything violent to you. And I mean it," he said softly. "But I'm scared I'm going to make myself crazy over you and drag you down with me. It made me crazy this morning in your office when you walked out. I would have stood in front of your building every day until I found you. If we start this again, I'm afraid I won't be able to leave you alone."

As he spoke, his hand tightened around my waist, his fingers pressing into my skin. "I'm scared as hell of how much I want to be with you. And we're just getting started. Yes, it made me hard as hell to hold you down in Paris. I wanted to have you and never let you go."

He let out a little groan and his intense eyes blazed into mine. He reached down to adjust himself, and his breaths were coming faster. "I'm afraid of how intense this feels. And if I messed up and you left me, I don't know what the fuck I'd do. I'll break both of our hearts because I won't be able to stop myself."

My fingers shook as I touched the bare skin of his arm. It was too much to take in. Jonas hadn't hidden this side of himself from the start. He was intense, and he told me from the beginning that he got hooked on things. Like me. In the bedroom, it was intense. The best kind of intense. But beyond? This was the other side of that intensity, the side that could be much more destructive. I just hadn't thought I'd be around long enough to decide if I could handle it.

Jonas looked away and took an uneven breath. "I've thought this through over and over since I left Paris, and I can't see any way this could end well. Not for me, not for you."

"But you still came," I whispered.

He nodded. "I still came. I'm walking right into the fire, too. I know it. And I still don't want to turn back."

I studied the creases of his forehead, waiting until he met my eyes. He held my gaze, and the electricity between us sizzled hotter. There were no questions in this area. Without our clothes, we could find our way back to each other. And then some. I was about to take another roller coaster ride to the heights of pleasure, of intimacy, knowing that lowest dips of loneliness would follow after he left. We were both getting sucked into our own sexual magnetic field, faster and faster into each other the longer he stayed.

When he wove his hand into my hair, I let out a long sigh of relief. My body had certainly decided, even if my rational brain was still on the fence.

"But I'll try as hard as I can not to mess this up. Just being here in this apartment with you is everything I've ever wanted. Everything I thought I'd never find," he whispered. "If I can't stop myself from fucking up, then there really is no hope for me. Ever."

He looked away, the corners of his mouth turned down.

"I missed you," I said. "I barely know you, and still I ached for you."

He turned back to me, his eyes filled with hope. Then his mouth came down on mine. It wasn't a kiss. It was a release of aching need, the same need that had been stirring in me all day, the kind of need that had led me to Jonas's hotel. Raw. Hungry. And threatening to spiral out of control.

So I let it.

I reached under his t-shirt and grabbed onto the hard, hot muscles of his stomach. God, he felt so good, so right. He groaned, and he moved to my neck, his teeth scraping against my skin. I gasped.

"Fuck," he mumbled. "I'm about to come, and we still have our clothes on."

I smiled. "Then let's take them off."

He let me go, and I took a step back, still breathless. He lifted off his shirt, revealing the display of muscles, scars and tattoos. Words, dark creatures, designs, all parts of him. How many times had I gotten myself off to the memory of this view? Finally, tonight, he wasn't just a memory.

"I want you, Alice," he whispered. "Badly. Here, on your tiny bed with too many pillows. I want to kiss you and hold you and make you come until the wary look on your face disappears."

My breaths came faster.

181

He cupped my cheeks. "So take off your clothes."

My heart was pounding so fast that it was hard to think. I turned around, brushing my shoulder against him, and whispered, "Unzip my dress, please."

A soft rumble came from deep in his chest, and he moved my hair to the side. His warm fingers brushed against my skin and he lowered the zipper. His movements slowed, sending a shiver of anticipation through me. He kissed the nape of my neck as he guided the dress over my shoulders with his rough fingertips.

His hands were gentle, intimate. I bit my lip. Was this more than I was ready for?

The dress slid down my body into a pool at my feet. His hands fumbled with the clasps of my bra until they released. He guided the little straps off my shoulders. Then he reached around to cup my breasts with his big hands and squeezed. A jolt of hard pleasure ran through me.

The buckle of his belt scraped against my back. I peeled off my silky stockings, bending forward to lower them, giving him a view. He rested his hand on my hips, positioning himself behind me.

"We haven't done this yet," he said, his voice tight, his erection hard against me. "But not now. Not this time."

I stood up, dressed only in my panties. I turned around and grabbed onto his belt. "So you still want to tell me how this will go between us?"

He furrowed his brow. "What do you mean?"

I pulled the leather through the buckle and set it free. Slowly, I unbuttoned his jeans.

"There are things I want, too," I said softly.

He froze. His eyes flickered up to mine, dark and intense. "Nothing rough."

I shook my head. "No, nothing like that." I frowned a little. "I won't ask that of you, Jonas."

He nodded, and his shoulders came down a bit. His gaze went back to my hands as they ventured lower. He ran his fingers down the back of my neck and leaned his forehead against mine.

"Then whatever you want," he whispered.

I smiled a little. Now that I'd asserted myself, I wasn't all together sure what to do. But one of the things I had thought about since Paris was how much he had guided every step of our little romance, both in and out of the bedroom. Even when I had tried to take the reins that last night, he found a way to take them back. Not that I blamed him, not anymore. Not after reading about his twisted relationship where that kind of play had gotten out of hand.

Jonas had been exceptionally good at reading me, even from the start. As the wariness disappeared from his face, I finally understood where he had learned this skill. His book was filled with details about the manipulative games he and his ex-girlfriend played, though the word *games* hardly described the dark twists they sometimes took. Jonas wrote about his ex-girlfriend's downward spiral into drugs, and he got better and better at reading her erratic moods, finding ways to out-maneuver her and keep control of the situation. Of her.

I frowned. Just like he out-maneuvered me that last night in Paris. Not that I was complaining about the results. But after all those dark years, he had built a life around dodging his triggers. Would he ever let his guard down?

So far, he had been in control of where each of our encounters went, and it turned me on. But looking back on our magical days together, he never once let me get him off, not even when I got down on my knees and asked. Would he give up some of that control, now that I knew a little more about his vulnerabilities? Did he trust me enough to let go, just for a bit?

I slipped my hand in his and led him to my bed. He sat down, the fly of his jeans open, his erection straining hard against his boxer briefs. I rested my hands on his shoulders and sat down to straddle him, shifting closer so I pressed up against his hard length. He kneaded my hips with his strong hands, and each breath came faster than the last.

We had sat like this on the first night in Stockholm, eye to eye, kissing, touching for the first time. When everything was new, when I had no idea what a night with Jonas would be like. So much had changed.

I traced the path of a scar along his torso. I had studied his tattoos in the bed and later in the bath in Paris, intricate stories he had chosen. But what about the marks he hadn't chosen? Some of the tattoos hid scars.

But one look at Jonas's face suggested that talking about his past was the last thing on his mind. His lips were parted, and the dark, hungry look in his eyes had a desperate edge. He was holding himself back, waiting.

So I kissed him. I pressed my mouth against his warm, soft lips, and his whole body reacted. His arms closed around me, his erection throbbed, pressed between us, and he let out a low rumble of a sigh. I tasted his bottom lip, exploring the contrast of stubble. His arms tensed, but he let me take my time, relearning, remembering. I opened my mouth, and he welcomed me deeper, reminding me of everything I had tried to forget these last months. Everything he made me want. Skin against skin.

"You're so beautiful," he groaned. "I can't believe this is real."

I moved slowly, my breasts pressed against the coarse hairs of his chest. He came in for another kiss, hungrier, and I dug my fingers into his shoulders as a ripple of pleasure shot through me.

God, he felt good, all that muscle and warmth enclosing me. It had been so, so long, and I couldn't get close enough. I threaded my hands through his thick hair and tilted my mouth for a better fit, looking for more. His tongue stroked mine, and I could no longer hold back the thoughts I had pushed away all these months. That I could fall in love with this man if I wasn't careful. That I was in so deep with him, drowning.

But if I drowned, I was going to bring him down with me. I pulled back, shifting until my feet found the floor. He stood up, all six-plus feet of half-naked man, waiting. With my eyes on his, I kneeled down in front of him. His eyes narrowed, and his hands clenched into fists.

"Fuck," he muttered. "I've made myself come so many times imagining you like this."

A bolt of heat rushed through me, strong and unmistakable. If I hadn't made a point of it, he would have certainly taken over control by now. And I liked this about him.

His fly hung open, and his erection pressed hard against the material of his boxers. Slowly, I slid his jeans down his muscular legs. He sat down on the bed and slipped them off, along with his socks. He rested his forearms on his thighs and looked up at me.

"This is getting close to torture, Alice," he said, his voice hoarse. "I'm about to get myself off just watching you. So what are we doing?"

I slipped my fingers under the elastic of the last piece of clothing he wore. "I want to be on top this time. I want to watch you enjoy it."

His eyes widened. "That's what you want?"

"Have you ever done that before?" I asked. "Have you ever just lay back and enjoyed it?"

He furrowed his brow, and the corners of his mouth turned down. "That's not usually how it goes for me."

I motioned for him to stand up again, and I inched the material over his hips. I eased it over his long, hard length. Wow. He was big. I knew that, but it still sent a hot shiver down my back.

"Did you bring a condom?" I asked.

He picked up his jeans and reached into the back pocket. "I grabbed a couple when I got the earrings from my hotel room. Just in case things went well."

I smiled. "And things are going well now?"

He smoothed my hair. "Well doesn't even begin to describe it."

I eased his boxer briefs further down, my mouth so close to his hard length.

"How would you describe it?" I whispered.

His hands slowed, the strokes through my hair turning to caresses. His expression turned serious. "Life-altering."

5

I STILLED, BLINKING up at him. He was no longer waiting for my move. Before I had played out the scene with him on the bottom, he was laying out his cards.

I eased his boxers down his legs. He stepped out of them and waited, staring down at me. Even when he was waiting for me to lead, he still had the air of tight control. His body itself was a reminder that he could settle any power struggle in the most basic of ways. But he didn't. He waited. Though his bobbing erection was much less patient than the rest of him.

I rested my hands on my thighs. His eyes flared with a rush of dark heat. I shifted, my mouth only a hair's distance from his hard length. But, no, not tonight.

I stood up, and Jonas let out something between a laugh and a groan.

"This is killing me," he said, shaking his head.

I pulled my pillows off the bed, dropping them onto the floor. "Let's lie down."

He raised an eyebrow and turned to pull the covers off my bed. He sank his long body onto my mattress and leaned back, his hands behind his head. He took up most of my narrow bed, looking like some kind of Nordic god, battle worn but still ready for anything. The corners of his mouth turned up into an amused smile.

"So you want me to just lie back and enjoy this?"

I nodded. "That's the idea."

I climbed onto the bed and straddled his legs. His smile faded, and his eyes blazed hotter. His gaze fell to my lips, then down further, over my shoulders, to my breasts.

"You look incredible," he said. "Did I tell you that yet tonight?"

I shook my head slowly.

"You do." He smiled. "Like from a dream. A really dirty one."

I slid my hands slowly up his body, over the scar along his left side. It was lined with the marks from stitches, unnaturally smooth. I'd ask about it later. If there was a later.

I moved higher and eyed the condoms he had set on the table. For once, I was setting the pace, and it was harder than I thought.

The truth was that I was just as inexperienced leading as he was at following.

"Something wrong?" Jonas's voice startled me out of my thoughts.

I shook my head. "Just trying to make sense out of all this."

He rested his hands on my thighs, his fingers brushing softly over my skin. "Sometimes none of it makes sense."

"Maybe." I smiled a little. "But this is what I'm wondering: What does a man who's scared of his own past want the most in bed?"

His blue eyes flickered with something dark before he closed them. I stretched out over his body, resting my elbows on the bed by his sides, and brushed a kiss on the frantic pulse throbbing at the base of his neck. No one on earth tasted this good. His breath hitched as I moved my kiss to his neck.

His hands moved up and down my body in light strokes. "I want someone who sees enough good in me that she brings me back to her apartment and lies naked with me and helps me remember why this is a life worth living." His voice was rough with emotion. "I want someone who trusts me, even when I don't trust myself."

My breath stopped at these words, and tears welled in the corners of my eyes. He wanted me. Not just the explosive sex. Everything.

The sadness and isolation of all these years must have been devastating. He had hinted at it before, but only now did I truly register how very, very lonely he was. And how much I wanted to help ease that burden.

How did I keep missing his point? This wasn't about what Jonas wanted in bed, and it never had been.

He gave me what I wanted in bed in hopes to find what he was aching for. A chance at something more. A chance to find real redemption.

I shifted to hold his face in my hands, but I didn't know what to say. I just stared into his deep blue eyes. They were a stormy bottomless ocean, and I couldn't pull myself away. I no longer wanted to. Nothing else in the world mattered. Just Jonas and me.

His erection pressed hard against my stomach, breaking the spell. Jonas frowned a little, but the lines disappeared when I stroked his cheek.

"Are you ready?" I whispered.

He chuckled. "I've been hard for you every single day since we left Paris."

A heavy rush of pleasure coursed through me. "What did you imagine?"

He closed his eyes and shook his head. "This is better."

I reached for the condom and sat back on my heels to tear it open. Jonas watched me intently as I eyed it.

"You know," I said, "I've never actually put one of these on a guy before you. But I practiced once on a banana in sex ed."

Jonas laughed. "You want some help?"

I shook my head and went to work. Jonas's smile disappeared as I touched his plump head. His long length was impossibly hard, and he groaned as my fingers worked their way down. It was so personal. By leaving this part to the guy every time, I had missed how intimate the act could be. There were a lot of things I had missed.

I finished rolling down the condom and slid my core against his length. I was just as ready as he was. I had been since he kissed me on the rainy sidewalk hours ago.

Jonas gave me a strained smile.

I positioned myself over him and pressed down, inch by inch. I was so unbearably full with him, so lost in the pleasure of this man. My breath hitched, and tears of relief threatened. His fingers clutched my hips, and he tilted his head back, teeth gritted. The thick muscles of his chest strained, moving the inked lines that covered him.

I raised myself up and sank down again. His fingers flexed against my hips, and he thrust hard. I cried out, and he did it again. If he kept this up, it wouldn't take long. I could lose myself again in his hard, hungry rhythm. Even from underneath me, he was taking back control. But no matter how good it felt, I wasn't going to let him. Not this time.

I wrapped my fingers around his muscular forearms and tugged.

"I'm in charge, remember?" But I didn't sound in charge at all. The words came out as a breathy plead.

He shook his head. "Not this time. Otherwise I can't wait for you."

I tugged at his hands again. "I don't want you to."

He stilled, and his expression was unreadable. I pulled once more on his arms, and he let go. I laced my fingers with his. Then I began to move again, finding a rhythm, losing myself in the delicious pressure. A pained look crossed his face. I let go of his hands and braced myself against the planes of his chest. His palms traveled over my body, caressing, squeezing. He found my breasts and held them with each palm, rubbing his thumbs over my nipple, his mouth parted.

"Fuck," he bit out. "Slow down or I'll come too soon."

I smiled and shook my head. "Then come."

I gasped in a breath as he thickened even more inside me. It was getting hard to speak. Deep lines cut across Jonas's brow, and he winced, somewhere between agony and ecstasy. But he wouldn't let go.

I slowed, and he squeezed his eyes shut and grimaced as his erection throbbed inside me, begging for more. Maybe this wasn't such a good idea. I hadn't meant to taunt him, just get a little taste of what this was like. The course of my life had been steered far too many times by a man jockeying for advantage. Was there room for my own will on this road to intimacy with Jonas?

I drew out each movement of my hips. His breaths were coming fast and hard, and a thin sheen of sweat covered his forehead. He gritted his teeth, fighting it, waiting for me.

"I want this, Jonas," I breathed. "I want to see you let go."

He looked at me, his gaze filled with hazy wonder, as if he finally understood what I was asking.

I started to move again, slowly at first, but the urgency on Jonas's face told me to go faster. He didn't look away. He looked straight at me, letting me see each surge of pleasure, each shudder. Every vulnerability was written on his face as I slowed again. He didn't take over. Warmth spread from the center of my stomach. He was finally giving himself over to me. My heart leapt as more pleasure flowed through me.

I grabbed his shoulders and came down hard, filling myself with him over and over. He roared, and his body seized, jackknifing up as he came hard inside me. His fingers dug into my waist, and he pulled me against him, his hips thrusting over and over.

His movements slowed, and he brought me down to the bed with him, his arms still around me. His breaths were harsh in my ear. I lay my palm on his neck, and his pulse throbbed under my fingers. I closed my eyes and rested on his chest as it rose and fell in a heavy rhythm.

Jonas kissed the top of my head and shifted out from under me. He slid off the bed and headed for the bathroom with the condom in his hand.

I rolled onto my back and looked up at the ceiling. He had given himself to me. He gave what I asked for. What came next? I had no experience in this area.

I turned to find Jonas leaning in the doorway, watching me. His eyes were heavy with desire, and he was already half hard again. Caught staring, his mouth curved up.

"In all these months, I haven't forgotten for one minute how good it feels to be with you," he said, his voice low. "It's driving me crazy that you haven't come yet."

He walked across the room and climbed back on the bed with me. The mattress dipped as he sank down next to me, gathering me in his arms. His growing erection pressed heavily between us.

"Did you get what you wanted, Alice?" he asked, slowly stroking my hair. "Or are you still looking for something else?"

I took a deep breath of his musky, familiar scent. Warmth grew in the pit of my stomach and spread through my body as I took another breath. And another. I no longer knew what I was looking for.

He raised himself over me, kissing my lips, my neck, my collar bone. He moved slowly down my body, his lips making a path over my breasts and onto my stomach. He was taking over again, and, God, it felt so good.

But tonight was supposed to be about something else.

"Wait," I said, my voice breathless.

"Please," he said. "Let me. It'll be good."

I had no doubts about that. But I grabbed his arms and looked into the bright blue depths of his eyes.

Lines creased his forehead. "If I can't give you this, what else do I have?"

"What else do you think that I want?" I asked quietly.

I traced the lines on this face. He closed his eyes at my touch.

"Someone who would never do the awful shit I've done," he whispered.

I sighed. In a way, he was right. I never wanted to go down the same path as my mother did. He was everything I didn't want. But maybe I was wrong about myself, too.

I stroked his cheek until he opened his eyes. "I want you, Jonas."

The lines faded from his forehead, and his eyes blazed with more than just desire. I bit my lip. I was in way too deep.

"I can make you feel so good." He kissed lower on my stomach. "Let me, Alice."

I had wanted to set our path tonight. But now he was staring at me like there was nothing else in the world he wanted more than to give my pleasure. I took a deep breath and nodded.

"Okay." His breath whispered over my skin as his lips teased, moving lower. He kissed me everywhere. On my hip bones. On my thighs. He let out a long breath that traveled over my sensitive skin, and I squirmed.

"You know what I've missed?" he asked.

I laughed. "Sex?"

Jonas shook his head and chuckled. "I was going for something a little classier than that." He stroked my thigh, and his smile faded. "I missed this feeling right now. That I'm going to do something that you'll love. That I can do that for you. And when I do you'll look at me like I'm exactly what you want."

I swallowed a lump in my throat and rested my hand on top of his. But before I could find the words to answer, he lowered his head and his warm mouth found every sensitive part of me. I moaned. It had been so long. I sucked in a breath and twisted, but his big hands wrapped around my thighs, holding me in place.

He circled and teased and buried his head between my legs. It was heaven. He used his mouth and his fingers to please me, reminding me of so many reasons why he was exactly what I wanted.

"You're making me so hard," he whispered against me, sending shivers through me. "All those little moans and shudders."

I was too worked up to respond, too worked up to think. All I wanted was more. He swirled his tongue and sucked until I cried his name.

"Oh, Jonas."

Pleasure pulsed through my body, and I shuddered and shook as he held me.

"Yes," he groaned. "Yes."

He rose up, his erection full again. He came down next to me, wrapping his arms around me. His long length pulsed against me. I would have welcomed sex again, but he didn't make any move to start. He just held me against him, his hand gliding up and down my back.

My breaths slowed, and I pulled back a little, stroking the line of his jaw. He had shaven that morning for the meeting, and the scar stood out against the ruddiness of his cheeks. It zigzagged up under his jaw at the end, stopping just before a pulsing artery. I had pictured his face so many times these last months, but I hadn't thought about how close that knife had come to doing much more harm.

"Is life still lonely for you?" I asked.

He raised his eyebrows. "In Stockholm?"

I nodded.

Jonas kissed my neck and took a deep breath, as if he were breathing *me* in. "Even lonelier than before." He raised his head again and added, "Or maybe I just notice it more now."

I brushed my fingers over the tattoo of the bird with the broken wing on his chest. "Is this you, flying into nothing?"

He stilled. "I guess it is," he finally said.

I rested my hand over the bird, covering it, cradling it. We lay still for a while, not saying anything.

Jonas shifted toward me, holding my hand against his chest. "I want you to come stay with me."

"Come to Sweden?"

He nodded.

I frowned. "I don't have that kind of money."

"I'll pay for your ticket."

I narrowed my eyes and shook my head. "You can't just pay for my plane ticket."

"Why not?"

"Because you already bought me earrings. You can't just keep buying me expensive things."

He raised an eyebrow. "I can buy you whatever the hell I want."

I sighed. "And I don't have any vacation time."

"None?"

I looked away. "Boars and Allen buys out my unused vacation days at the end of the year. And I need the money."

His eyes narrowed. "No holidays?"

"The office closes between Christmas and New Year's."

"Oh," he said, grimacing. He rubbed his forehead and let me go, rolling onto his back. "Look, don't get me wrong. I really want you to come. But I don't make the best company around the Christmas holiday."

"Why?"

"I really don't like it."

"Like Scrooge and the Grinch?" I wrinkled my forehead. "You know who they are, don't you?"

"Yes, I know who they are." Jonas gave a little snort. "I'm like the Grinch."

"What do you do on Christmas Day?"

He shook his head. "You don't want to know."

I squeezed my eyes shut against the surge of frustration that rushed through me. What? He was telling me not to come at Christmas, with no explanation? Why was he holding back this time?

I broke away from the warmth of his arms and rolled off the bed. It was too hard to think when I was so close to him. I headed for the kitchen and got a glass of water.

It kept coming back to the same thing. He talked as if he wanted to work out a future together, but there was so much he held back. Was he what I wanted or what I feared the most? Or both?

This time, I wasn't going to let it go. I set down my glass and started back for my bed. And for Jonas. I was very naked now as I walked back to him, as his gaze slid down my body, alive, electric.

I sat down on the edge of the mattress. My bed was so narrow that it was impossible not to brush up against him.

"All that talk in the park about how into me you are, about going too far," I said. "How can you say that when I'm not even welcome for Christmas?"

Jonas winced. The look on his face was so pained that I almost backed down, almost told him to forget about it. Almost.

He muttered something under his breath and shook his head. He rested his hand on my leg. "Come for New Years instead."

After all the intimacy on this little bed, he was maneuvering me away from the areas where he didn't want me. And he was so good at it.

"I don't know if I can do that," I said.

The hand on my thigh tensed, and then it was gone. He sat up behind me and kissed my shoulder. "Lie with me, Alice."

I wasn't sure I wanted to lie next to him. If I did, I was afraid he'd be able to talk me into just about anything.

He eased me down so my head rested on his shoulder, my cheek on his warm skin, his scent everywhere. His chest rose and fell, his tattoos moving, alive.

"Come see me and I'll tell you everything," he whispered. "My father. My mother. All the things I left out of the book."

I said nothing.

"We have so little time here." His arms tightened around me. "You don't have to answer right now. I'll write you letters."

I frowned. "Like with pen and paper?"

"Yes. That kind." Soft breaths of laughter brushed over me.

"I don't think I'll make a very good pen pal," I said. "I've never written letters to anyone."

"You don't have to," he said. "Just read mine, and if you still see something you want with me, then come. I'll pay. The two of us for New Years. A real start."

I didn't answer. Had my brain already made this decision, too? When he rolled onto his side and pressed the length of his body against mine, I couldn't resist any longer. My heart fluttered with the kind of hope that should have died years ago. But it hadn't.

Jonas brushed my hair off my face. His eyes were sparkling, dark, and bottomless, filled with promises I wanted to believe.

He kissed me once, twice, letting his full lips linger against mine. "If it's this good between us, we'll find a way."

REDEMPTION

1

THE TAXI SKIDDED around the corner, onto a slushy side street in Södermalm. The car stopped in front of a nondescript entrance along a long brick building. I opened the door and stepped out into the cold. Somewhere along the ride from the airport, the sun had set, though it was only early afternoon. The streetlights glowed, and the sidewalk was padded with a thin layer of newly fallen snow.

The taxi driver set my little suitcase on the curb and took off, leaving me to fend for myself in front of Jonas's building. I looked one way down the empty street, then the other. What were the chances of getting another taxi on Christmas Eve in Stockholm if he wasn't home? Or if he slammed the door in my face? Maybe I should have just done things his way and taken him up on his plane ticket offer. But then the visit would be on his terms. Again.

Jonas made it clear I shouldn't come for Christmas, and he still hadn't told me why. So I had come anyway. On Christmas Eve. In case he was serious enough about his anti-Christmas stance that I needed to find a hotel room. Not that finding a room would be easy on a night like this.

And if I ruined everything between us by pushing back against his limits? It was better to know that now, before we got in deeper. If my mother had stood up for what she wanted years earlier, maybe her life wouldn't have ended up such a mess.

I scanned the windows of the building in front of me, lit with stars, lights and electric candles. Which apartment was Jonas's? His letters had described a view of a courtyard, but there was no courtyard in sight. Just a quiet wall of brick with windows in neat rows. Maybe this wasn't even the right place. I pulled out my phone, checked the address one more time, and took a deep breath. Showtime.

A cold gust of wind wrapped around my bare hands, seeping through my jeans and finding its way into my boots. Best to just get this over with.

I dialed Jonas's number.

"Alice?"

"Um, hi," I said.

The line was silent.

"Alice. It's you," he finally said. "Is everything okay?"

His voice sounded strange, off, and his accent was more pronounced than I remembered.

I took a deep breath. "I have a bit of a surprise for you."

"What is it?"

The words came out all slurred together. Something was definitely off. If my feet weren't currently numbing over, I might have even turned around.

"I'm here in Stockholm," I said.

He muttered something incomprehensible, and then the line went silent. Did he hang up on me? I checked the screen of my phone. No, he was still there.

"Where are you?" He didn't sound the least bit happy to hear from me. Maybe even mad.

Well, what was I expecting? It was better that I found this out right away. How many times had I told myself that today?

"Alice?" His voice was softer now. "Where are you?"

"In front of your building."

Another long pause, then a heavy breath came through the phone. "Okay."

Okay, goodbye or *okay, I'll be right there*? He wasn't buzzing me in, but maybe the doors here in Sweden worked differently. I was starting to shiver. Where did I pack my hat and gloves? In the bottom of my suitcase, no doubt. If I opened it to search, a week's worth of socks would probably fall into the snow. I hadn't quite planned for this.

The door to the building opened, and there he was. Unshaven, dressed in a wrinkled t-shirt that left plenty of the tattoos on his biceps visible. His boots were untied, and one side of his hair stood on end, as if he had just rolled out of bed. Or hadn't looked in the mirror.

Jonas stared at me for a moment, then swiped his hands over his eyes. He took a couple steps forward, stopping inches away. He raised his hand and touched my hair tentatively, as if he were making sure I was really there. His fingers brushed over my cold cheeks, and he winced. Yes, I was real. And freezing.

He blew out a long breath and the scent of whiskey hit me hard. I stiffened. I'd know that scent anywhere. But Jonas didn't drink. Or at least he hadn't around me. Before I could think further, he wrapped his arms around me in a clumsy embrace.

"What the fuck are you doing here today?" he whispered, pulling back a little. His jaw was tense, and his eyes flashed with anger, but he didn't let go.

"I know you said not to come for Christmas, and clearly you have reasons for that." I gave him a pointed look. "But what if that's what I really wanted? You wouldn't even discuss it with me. So I came a day early to talk about it in person."

"To see what I'd do?" The creases on his forehead grew deeper.

I frowned. "If you didn't want—"

"We celebrate Christmas on the twenty-fourth, not the twenty-fifth," he said, cutting me off.

"Oh," I whispered. I had meant to force his hand, but not quite like this.

Jonas's arms tightened around me again, pulling me closer and closer. He didn't seem to notice the icy gusts of wind blowing down the street, and he still hadn't invited me in.

"Sorry," I said into his chest. "This wasn't what I meant to do. I would have come earlier in the week, but I had to work."

Jonas made a sound that was somewhere between pain and laughter.

"I'll find a hotel," I said.

Jonas's whole body tensed, his arms locked around me. "Hell no. You're not leaving now."

He leaned down so his lips brushed against my ear. The scent of whiskey and Jonas was startling and so, so good. Shit.

"You wanted this, Alice, so come on upstairs." His voice was low and seductive, leaving no question about what would happen if I said yes. "Or have I finally scared you off?"

It was a challenge.

He rocked a little to the side. There were all sorts of things the drinking could mean, most of them not good. In Jonas's book, it was his ex-girlfriend who got too deep into drinking and drugs, not him. So why the hell was he drunk at two in the afternoon on Christmas Eve?

But there was pain in his deep blue eyes as he stared down at me, waiting for my answer. I had flown all the way from New York to start something real. And this was about as real as it got.

My heart thumped in my chest. Was I about to make the stupidest decision of my life? This wasn't the first time I had asked myself this question around him.

I swallowed. "I'd be an idiot not to be scared right now."

Jonas just raised his eyebrows.

I reached for my suitcase, balanced on the slushy sidewalk, but he took it out of my hand and started for the door of the building. Inside was a small hallway with marble floors and long rows of mailboxes. Jonas gestured to the door at the end of the hall. "My apartment is through the courtyard."

His letters always mentioned the courtyard in some way. The color of the leaves on the trees. The stone path that crossed through the grass, to his door. Now I could see how it worked. Through the hall, another door opened into a large, rectangular enclosure. As the door closed behind me, the din from the city disappeared. The space was larger than I had imagined, and the trees and the bench were all blanketed in a thin layer of untouched snow. He had written snippets about his glimpses into the apartment windows that surrounded us on every side. Today some were lit with the same kinds of stars and candles I had seen from the street.

The whole scene would have been magical if Jonas weren't fucking drunk.

He reached the door to the building and held it open for me. Still a gentleman, even in this state. Though that might not last when we got to his apartment.

He pushed the elevator call button, and we rode up to the fourth floor in silence. Our steps echoed in the bland hallway. Much nicer than my own in New York, but other than our footsteps, the place was silent, as if no one else lived there. Jonas stopped in front of one of the apartments, fumbling with his keys. The heavy wooden door swung open, and I stepped in.

My fingers were still numb and clumsy from the cold as I unbuttoned my coat. I shivered as I slipped it off.

He took the heavy jacket from me, but he didn't hang it up right away. He swept my hair off my neck, and I closed my eyes. Was he going to kiss me? His hot breaths came fast in my ear. I stilled, waiting, my heart thumping hard in my chest. This could go any number of ways.

But then he was gone. I opened my eyes.

"The place is a little bare," he said, nodding into his living room.

He wasn't kidding. The living room was larger than my New York studio, but from the little hallway where I stood, all I could see was an old, wooden desk under one of the windows. I walked in, and Jonas followed close behind, the dark cloud of his presence everywhere. The desk was bare except for a notebook. No computer, no laptop.

"You write by hand?" I asked.

He nodded. "It works better that way for me. It's a habit from when I was in prison. Now I just think better when I have a pen in my hand."

Right, prison. Because he had put more than one person in the hospital. I had come to terms with this piece of him, hadn't I?

Next to the desk, along the wall was a low shelf filled with books. In the middle of the room was a black sofa in pristine condition, with a half-empty bottle of whiskey in front of it. Nothing on the walls, no rugs. If he hadn't written this room into his letters, I would have guessed he never used it.

I sat down and patted the pillows. "Not many guests?"

He shook his head.

"I bought the sofa a few days ago. For your New Year's visit," he added dryly.

I ignored the jab. He stood in the entryway, arms crossed, watching me, his eyes blazing.

I picked up the bottle next to my feet. "I didn't know you were a Maker's Mark kind of guy."

His eyes narrowed, and his jaw tightened. "It's a family tradition."

"Why the hell are you drunk at two in the afternoon on Christmas Eve?"

"I already told you," he said softly. "It's tradition."

That was all he had to say on the subject? Jonas had mentioned his father's drinking in New York, and I was getting a more personal introduction to that detail now. But he still wouldn't explain? Yes, I had come today without an invitation. But if I hadn't, when would he have told me about this?

And what was he planning for the rest of his day?

"Ready for the next room?" he asked.

"No, I'm not ready for the next room," I snapped. "What's going on here?"

"You keep hold of your past just as tightly as I do," he muttered. "Is that why you came? To see if I'm too much of a fuck-up for you to handle?"

"Don't be such an ass about this, Jonas. You're drunk and alone on December twenty-fourth." I swallowed back a sudden lump in my throat. "I came here for you."

He winced. The alcohol seemed to loosen up that tight control he held over his reactions whenever we got into more difficult territory. Finally, I could read his face, though this might not be the best day for it. Angry. Sad. Maybe something else. His Adam's apple bobbed as he swallowed.

In slow steps, he crossed the room. He sank down next to me on the sofa and rested his forearms on his thighs. Jonas had sat that way, staring at the floor in front of him, when he told me about his jail time back in Paris.

He seemed to be working himself up to speak, and I waited, giving him all the time he needed. Maybe I knew him better than I thought.

"What do you want me to say?" he asked.

I shrugged. "I want to know why. Why the hell is this a family tradition?"

We sat in silence on the couch for a long time. He was bent over like a wounded animal, and I was cornering him about his past. He could either lash out or give in.

Jonas took a deep breath and blew it out. "My father likes Maker's Mark more than anything or anyone in the world. So when my father wanted me to join him one Christmas Eve when my mother went off to church, it was that or stay out of sight."

Jonas grabbed the bottle of whiskey and took a drink. He grimaced and twisted the cap back on. "Best time I ever had with my father."

He ran a hand through his hair, another gesture I knew. Just saying these words was painful for him.

"My mother came home a few hours later, and something happened when she saw us together at the kitchen table with the bottle between us." His voice had quieted to a whisper. "It was like she finally understood who my father was and where I was headed. I don't think she ever really recovered."

A hundred questions reeled through my mind in the silence of his bare living room, but I hesitated. What kind of pain would each of my questions cause? Though his current state suggested he was already suffering, whether he told the story or not.

"How old were you when this happened?" I asked.

"Fifteen."

And he had carried the weight of this moment on his shoulders ever since.

"And you've celebrated Christmas like this for the last sixteen years?"

"Most of them," he said, glancing over at me. "I call him up on Christmas Eve, and we talk a little and drink. And when he's no longer making much sense, I say goodbye."

"And your mother?"

"We don't speak around the holidays anymore. Her choice." He grimaced. "At least she doesn't live with my father anymore."

I rubbed my forehead. "Is this holiday ritual another one of your self-inflicted punishments?"

He ran his hand through his hair a couple more times. "Maybe."

"How many years until you've served your time for this one?"

Finally, Jonas turned to me. "This is the last year. I turned down your offer to be together for Christmas to get drunk with my father. Something about how fucked up that choice is got through to me as I sat here this morning listening to my father go on about the guy who he thought stole money from him at the pub last weekend. Over and over, I thought, this is what I chose instead of Alice."

He was grinding his jaw, and there was an unsteady glimmer in his eyes. "Now you're here, and I'm drunk. I'm one step away from going down to the pub for a good fight."

"Because that would help?" I asked.

His eyes flared with a surge of heat. "That's one of two things that takes the edge off this kind of mood."

His gaze traveled down my body, making it clear what the other thing was. And how it would be. Not tender or full of the longing I ached with these last months. Jonas's gaze was crude, full of volatile lust. I couldn't have what I wanted from him. Would I settle for this instead?

He took an unsteady breath and turned away. "Ready for the rest of your tour now?"

2

I FOLLOWED HIM a few steps down the hallway into a sleek white kitchen. Dirty dishes were piled onto the counter. Half a plate of pasta with sauce and a few slices of garlic bread were on the table, long-forgotten. As if Jonas had been interrupted, mid-meal, when his father had called.

"Not as clean as your place," Jonas said with a smirk.

I walked further into the narrow room, over to the glass door at the other side. It opened onto a small balcony. "This is nice."

"I rarely use it," he said. "I used to smoke there, so it's easier just to stay away."

Used to smoke. So many things to stay away from. Smoking, drinking, fighting.

As I walked back to Jonas, an envelope caught my eye, propped up on the counter. It had my name on it, "Alice," underlined, in the same messy scrawl from Jonas's letters. I slowed until I stopped in front of it.

"This is for me?" I asked.

He scowled and looked away. "Not yet. Not like this."

In my own handbag, there was an envelope with Jonas's name printed neatly on it, too. But he was right. This was a bad time for letters or gifts or whatever was in there. I glanced once more at his envelope and headed out. He leaned against the doorway, his body blocking enough so I'd have to squeeze by him to pass. I slowed as I came closer. He pushed off the door jam, his body filling the whole space. His eyes were hot, and he shoved his hands into his pockets.

"Are we finishing the tour?" he asked, his voice low and sultry.

All that was left was the bedroom. Was I ready to walk into it? Jonas had a hungry, almost feral look to him now. If I said no, he'd let it be, and I'd probably spend the rest of my life wondering what would have happened next.

"Yes."

He took a step closer, backing me up against the wall. In case I didn't get his message the first time around, he was delivering it, loud and clear. He leaned over me and brushed my hair off my shoulder, the way he had in the hallway earlier. Slowly, he bent down, rested his lips on my neck, and took a deep breath.

"You smell so fucking good right now," he whispered in my ear.

He straightened up and turned down toward the bedroom. I slumped back against the wall, trying to slow my breaths.

"We'll skip the bathroom," he said over his shoulder. "It's a mess."

Jonas wandered on until he came to the last door. I caught up and brushed by him for a look. A wide bed with dark blue covers, unmade. Two free-standing closets. A set of weights, probably too big for me to lift. White walls, rolling blinds. It was serene and impersonal except for a t-shirt on the floor.

I turned to him. "It's empty in here."

Jonas shrugged. "I'm not sure what I'm supposed to fill it with."

I raised my eyebrows. If I had money, my apartment wouldn't look like this. "So you're just gathering heaps of royalties and putting them in the bank?"

His gaze softened. "Just waiting for something worthwhile to spend it on."

There was that word again, worthwhile. His gaze was so intense, driving home his last comment. He had used the word before when he told me about the prison librarian, who had seen something worthwhile in coming every week.

I thought maybe, when I got out, I could meet someone who might see something worthwhile in me.

I hadn't understood just how deep that idea ran through him. Had he spent the years since he got out of prison looking for something worthwhile? Waiting to find the answer before he started living life again?

Jonas had grown up without much money, just like me. If the contract with Boars and Allen was any indication, he could afford whatever he wanted, live however he wanted to make up for everything he missed. This is what he chose?

I walked through his bedroom, running my hand over the rumpled heap of his comforter, and stopped at the window. There wasn't a balcony from this room, but the sill was almost wide enough to sit on. I leaned into it for a view of the snowy courtyard and the apartments across from his.

I turned around. Jonas's eyes flared with scalding heat as he stared at me with hunger. That's what it was – endless hunger. No veneer of civilized restraint, no careful reading of my limits, just his own, unbridled want. And we were in his bedroom.

He started across the room for me in slow, deliberate steps. There was no mistaking what he was coming for.

"If you're going to run, Alice, this is your chance," he said. "I've already had a shitty day, and I'm feeling like a bitter, selfish bastard who will take whatever he wants."

This was what I had told myself I needed from him all this time. I needed to see him at his worst, to understand if I was making the same mistakes as my mother made. And it was about to go down, right now.

I straightened up and tilted my chin up to stare at him. "What do you want?"

He bent over me, his breath harsh in my ear. "Is that why you're here today? To dig up all the things I didn't want to talk about and see what happens? To see if I'll be the same kind of asshole your father was?"

Um, well, yes. But put so bluntly into words, it sounded pretty selfish.

"I didn't mean to come on the holiday itself, Jonas," I whispered.

He stopped right in front of me, but he didn't touch me. He rested his arm against the wall, and his big body hovered over me. "I thought I wanted to be left alone today, get drunk, just get through the day. But now that you're here, I want something else."

Something else was the part I should be worrying about, but it was the get through the day part that I clung to. Should I push him to say more? What would he do if I touched him? My fingers trembled as I reached for his arms. He sucked in a harsh breath.

"I can't tell you how many times I've imagined this, Alice," he whispered. "You in my bedroom. Under me. On your knees. And I'm drunk enough that I'm not going to hold back, even if it's a really bad idea right now."

These last words came out in a slurred jumble, and his muscles tensed under my fingers. Oh, God. This was it. The last chance to either decide if this – he – was too much, or ignore the red warning flags going off and see what it was that he wanted, needed when he was at his lowest. I had read about all the power games he played with his other red-headed girlfriend. Is that what he wanted from me? If it was, I wasn't sure if I was turned on or scared.

"You still want to be here with me, Alice?" His muscles twitched, but he still didn't touch me.

I ran my hands down his arms and slipped them under the hem of his t-shirt. His skin was hot, and his stomach flexed in quick erratic breaths. I had flown all the way from New York for this man. I still wanted him.

My hands wandered further down to the waistband of his jeans, but he grabbed them before I ventured further.

"Not like that," he said, a little colder. "On my bed."

I blinked up at him. Echoes of the hard expression from across the New York conference room table crossed his face. He was in that place again, the place he fought to stay away from.

He led me over to his bed and stood behind me. "I'm so fucking hard for you right now."

He pressed up behind, flexed his hips into my ass, crudely showing me exactly what he wanted.

I looked over my shoulder, into his piercing blue eyes. "Do it."

His hands tightened, and he let out a low hiss.

"Did you get tested?"

I nodded. He had told me he was getting tested in his letter and asked if I wanted to do the same. I never answered.

He groaned. "And you're clean?"

I nodded again.

"I am, too," he said. "So now we see what bare is like for us."

A twinge of sadness washed over me. I had imagined bare as a way to be closer with him, but that's not what this would be about. This wouldn't bring us closer. This was selfish relief, plain and simple. I wouldn't even see the look on his face. Maybe it was better that way.

"Do it, Jonas," I breathed.

He stilled behind me. Leaning his heavy body over mine, he kissed my neck softly. He stayed there for a long time, his breath reeking of alcohol and desperation. But the moment passed, and his hands returned to my hips. He slid his fingers over my stomach and unbuttoned my jeans.

"Fuck," he muttered as he tugged them down over my hips.

He reached between my legs and found what he was looking for. Despite everything that was off about this day, I wanted him. God, how I had missed him, the gut-wrenching honesty of each encounter.

And then there were the physical things I missed. I had thought I was above choosing a man because of his body, but with Jonas, I couldn't deny it was part of his appeal. The intricate tattoos that spread across the planes of his chest and down the thick, hard muscles of his arms. He still had the body of a fighter, despite everything that had happened, the muscles that tensed when I touched them.

And then there was the way he touched me. His ex-girlfriend may have twisted up his heart, but she had also taught him his way around a woman's body. How to make me feel good, how to make me feel like pleasure was some sort of secret only he held. I still hadn't quite come to terms with this part of him.

But Jonas was drunk and scowling, the dark cloud hovering, threatening to burst over us both. His belt buckle rustled behind me, then his zipper. After months apart, after all his beautiful letters, this was how he wanted it to be between us. No romance, no subtlety. He tugged my sweater off and dropped it on the ground unceremoniously. Then his back was up against mine, the scent of whiskey and sex surrounding me.

"Bend over onto the bed," he said, his deep, raspy voice in my ear. His hand guided me down. "Lower."

We had done all sorts of things together, but bent over his bed, I was exposed in a whole different way. In my bra, with my jeans around my thighs, it was the opposite of intimacy.

He pushed his long, thick length between my legs and teased me. He did it again and again, changing his angle, playing, until I met his strokes.

"On the bed," he groaned.

I shimmied out of my jeans and climbed up. He was right behind me, his legs spreading mine, his hands stilling my hips. One hand moved between my legs, and heat flooded to my cheeks. Yes, despite everything, I was turned on.

He slowed, his touch gentler.

"You still want me," he whispered, almost to himself. "Fuck."

He sucked in a long breath, and for a moment I thought he might back away, call this off. But his hand disappeared, and he positioned himself at my entrance and pushed hard.

For one moment, everything was right again. Everything else disappeared except the deep relief of Jonas finally inside me again, filling me. A guttural cry came from him, and he moved with a few, wild thrusts. I moaned, and he moved again, finding a hard, steady rhythm.

"You feel so good like this," he said through gritted teeth.

So much pleasure. He swirled his hips, his fingers tight around my waist. But I fought not to lose myself. Not like this. I looked over my shoulder. His eyes were closed, and his face was screwed into a tight grimace that bordered on pain.

"Jonas," I said, breathless, my heart breaking.

But he heard. He stopped at the sound of my voice.

"Oh, Alice," he whispered.

The regret in his voice hit me deep inside. Everything in me ached for him.

He shifted behind me, and his shirt dropped onto the bed. Then, gently, he guided my back, off my hands until I was on his lap, my legs spread, his erection still inside me. He held me against him so we were skin to skin. His lips pressed against the nape of my neck. His big hands wrapped around my arms, holding my tight.

"Oh, God, Alice." He groaned and shifted his hips, pushing deeper inside. "Why did you do this? Why the fuck did you have to come and see me like this?"

"I came because I want you, Jonas," I whispered.

It was the truth. Either we could handle this or we couldn't. In any other relationship we'd dance around the harder issues for months, years before we faced them. But this wasn't any other relationship. It was all or nothing with Jonas. Maybe it was that way with me, too.

His heavy body surrounded mine, and his breaths were hot and fast in my hair.

"Why won't you let me be here for you, Jonas?" I asked. "Is this all you want from me?"

His fingers flexed hard around my arms, his hot, angry breaths coming hard on my neck. "You know it's not true."

"I don't know anything right now."

Before I could think any further, he began to move again. His big hands slid down my arms. He found my hips and grabbed on. I raised up, and he pulled me down hard, thrusting deep enough to take my breath away. I could get lost in this feeling. Forget everything else that mattered. If we had reached Jonas's limits, at least I could have this feeling.

He muttered a few words in Swedish and lifted me again. This time, he thrust up to meet me, his breath hot on my shoulder. But the anger was gone now, the regret, too. Just that electric pull between us, that desperate search to come closer, to make every boundary between us disappear. His arm tightened around me, holding me against his hot, slick chest as he thrust, faster and faster. His breaths were short and erratic.

"I want you, Alice," he said, his voice thick with emotion. "Let me have you."

The words were laced with all kinds of need, and they hit deep down. The strain of his low voice echoed inside as pleasure erupted through me. I cried out, trembling, as he bucked and let himself go, coming hard inside me in three sharp thrusts. He wrapped his arms around me, holding me so tightly against him, sending waves of warmth through me, making this all into something more.

His arms loosened, and he kissed me softly, his mouth buried in my hair. My body was heavy, and my eyelids fluttered closed. I leaned forward, and Jonas followed behind me, lowering us to the bed, one arm still around me. Our breaths slowed, and I lay still, drifting off to a place where all the things that had happened that day made sense.

3

I WOKE UP with Jonas still half inside me. His arm was wrapped tightly around my waist, pressing my body into his. How long had I slept like that, tangled together with him? I lifted my head to look for a clock but found nothing. It was dark outside, but it had been when I arrived, too. Hunger gnawed at my stomach. Must be mealtime, at least according to my body's clock.

I shifted away from Jonas, but he snored softly and pulled me back into his arms. His erection grew, teasing, but I wasn't ready for that again. The haze of jetlag made everything even more surreal. I needed a little distance from the ease that flooded me, deep down, when his body was so close. Peeling back his heavy arm, I slipped away without looking back.

The bathroom was as promised. Messy. Not disgusting, just *I-don't-give-a-shit* messy. Toothpaste cap off. Toilet seat up. He probably had someone come and clean for him. A hot Swedish maid? I massaged my temples. Stupid line of thought.

I turned on the shower and let it warm up, slowly removing the last of my clothes. Maybe the water would help clear my head. I stepped in and let the hot streams run down my body.

There wasn't much in the way of identifiable products in Jonas's shower. I opened the caps, but they all smelled like men. Like Jonas. Maybe soap was the best bet.

As I rubbed the bar between my hands, the door opened. Jonas stood in the doorway, staring at me through the foggy glass of the shower stall. He was only half-dressed in jeans, and his hair stuck up on one side, worse than before. It would have been funny and cute in any other situation. He frowned and looked away.

"You can come in," I said.

It was a little late in the game for modesty.

Jonas's shoulders fell, and he entered. He lowered the toilet lid and sank down onto it. He rested his forearms on his heavy thighs. Still, after all that happened, I couldn't take my eyes off the broad expanse of his shoulders, the intricate tattoos that wove along the muscles. Apparently, this man could do whatever the hell he wanted, and I'd still think he was hot.

"Sobering up?" I asked.

"Some." His shoulders rose and fell. "I'm so sorry. About everything."

I said nothing, just washing the layers of travel and sex from my body. More steam clouded the shower stall, making Jonas a hazy fantasy.

"I should have talked to you about Christmas," he said quietly.

Yes. He should have.

I shut off the water. Jonas reached for a towel and opened the steamy shower door. He wrapped it around me and held me for an extra beat. He stroked my cheek and pulled my wet curls free from under the towel. The gesture was so tender, so intimate, and I closed my eyes against the warmth that flooded through me. Damn him for making me want to forget what had just happened so soon. And he still wasn't sober.

Was this the same roller coaster my mother had dedicated she life to?

I took a deep breath and opened my eyes. And stilled. On the formerly empty plane of his chest was a new tattoo. A bird, small, with hints of white along its graceful body. I hadn't seen it through the steamy glass of the shower stall, but now it stretched its wings in front of me. It was flying toward the other, older bird, the black one with the broken wing. If the scene played out, at least one of the two would need to switch directions or they'd collide. But neither of the two birds seemed to notice, not yet. They just flew toward each other.

In New York I had asked if the injured black bird flying away into nothing was him. Now, in this new tableaux, it was no longer flying away. I was trying so hard not to hope. And failing.

I untangled my hand from the towel and brushed my fingers over the design. The tattoo was still new, the lines raised.

The gentle rise and fall of Jonas's chest stopped. Slowly, I looked up until I came to the endless blue of his eyes. I waited for him to explain, my hand drifting down to the broken wing of the black bird.

"I must smell like hell," he said finally, looking away. "Let me get in the shower, sober up a little more."

I nodded and dropped my hand from his chest. Maneuvering around him, I leaned against the sink. His eyes widened.

"You're going to watch?" he asked.

I shrugged. "Why not?"

The corners of his mouth turned up. It was the first hint of a real smile I had seen.

"Why not," he echoed.

Jonas turned on the water. He shucked his jeans and boxers and stepped into the shower without a glance at me. The glass was still fogged, but not so much as to hide his movements as he washed. He turned to rinse, eyes closed, his hands in his hair, water running down his long, hard body.

Was he putting on a sexy show on purpose? If so, I had asked for it.

He shut off the shower and stepped out. My gaze flicked down before I could think better of it. For once, he wasn't hard, and it made his current state of undress more personal, a different kind of intimate.

I looked up quickly, but he had noticed. His eyebrows rose, and he smiled a little before grabbing the towel. The process was captivating. He rubbed his hair until it stuck out in all directions, then worked his way down his body. He had already caught me staring, so there was no reason to stop now. Scars and tattoos marred his skin, and he had a sort of wild, un-kept look about him, as if he were not fit for civilized company. But the whole scene was beautiful. I came all the way to Sweden to see this man, not some glossier version of him. At some point, I had to accept this part of myself.

Jonas finished drying off and looked up at me, the corners of his mouth turned up.

"Done looking?" he asked.

I shrugged, and his smile grew.

He wrapped the towel around his waist and nodded to the door. "I'll get dressed and find us something to eat. We need to talk."

I took my time drying off in the bathroom, waiting. When I heard Jonas's footsteps travel down the hall again, I hauled my suitcase into his room. He had cleaned up the clothes from the floor and made his bed. I sat down on the dark blue comforter as I tugged on a new pair of jeans. I slowed as I looked around the room. What was it like to be Jonas? He kept himself locked up in this bare apartment, as if he were still doing time.

I knelt down and dug around my suitcase for my brush and a little make-up. Jonas probably didn't own a hairdryer, so my look would be curly and wild. But at this point, my hair was the least of my worries.

I padded down the hall and slipped into the bathroom again to finish getting ready. By the time I faced him, I had to be ready to talk. Ready to decide how to make sense out of the fact that I was falling in love with a man who got drunk alone on Christmas Eve.

When I finally peeked around the corner into the kitchen, Jonas sat at the small, round table by the window, looking back at me.

"I got out some things for sandwiches," he said. "It's that or leftover take-out food."

I smiled. "Anything is fine. I'm starving."

Jonas had set out cheese, meat and other, less recognizable items along the counter. He came up behind me and handed me a plate.

"What's that?" I pointed to a tub of grayish-brown spread.

"Liver paste."

I raised an eyebrow. "You're kidding."

Jonas shook his head.

"Hmm... I think I'll play it safe for my first meal," I said. "Ham and cheese are the same over here, right?"

"Just about."

We moved around each other, fixing sandwiches, brushing against each other. Jonas slipped his hand around my hip as he reached for glasses, and I stilled at the warmth of him behind me. We had never had enough time to just be together. The short snippets of each visit hadn't given us the space for the quiet of getting ready for a meal. If I decided to stay, we could explore this during the week. If.

Jonas opened the door of the refrigerator and rummaged around a bit.

"Milk or water? Or whiskey?"

I stopped, turning to him. He studied my face, carefully gauging my reaction.

"I was joking, Alice," he said softly.

My face burned. "Water's fine."

There were only two chairs at the table, and Jonas had pulled the second one next to his so that it faced the snowy window. It was dark outside, and most of the lights in the building were out. I sat down and took a bite of the sandwich. Damn, I was hungry.

"What time is it?" I asked.

"A little before midnight."

I blinked. "Whoa."

It was probably good we slept so long. He must be sober-ish by now.

I devoured my sandwich and stood up to make another. I studied the different breads lined up on the counter and chose the one that looked least like something I'd find in a New York grocery store.

As I reached for the mayonnaise, I looked up. Jonas was staring at me. There was the familiar hunger and longing in his gaze, but there was something else. Something new. Something that made me stop.

"Sorry," he said, shaking his head. "I just can't believe you're here."

"Is that good or bad?"

He sighed. "I think that's for you to decide at this point. I'm hoping it's good."

I sat down at the table and took a bite of my sandwich. The snow had begun to fall, and it shimmered in the darkness of the night.

"Here's the thing," said Jonas, breaking the stillness of this little kitchen scene. "I have a train ticket booked for early tomorrow morning."

"I see," I said, putting down the sandwich.

He ran a hand through his hair. "My father sounded even more paranoid than usual this morning. So after I had a long discussion with that bottle of whiskey, I bought a ticket up north to visit for a few days, just one last time." He gave me a pointed look and sighed. "I'm returning late on December thirtieth. In time for your arrival."

I nodded slowly. "How long has it been since you've seen him?"

"As soon as I started making money from my book, I bought my mother an apartment here in Stockholm," he said, frowning. "That didn't go over well."

"But you still talk to him?"

"Once a year." Jonas took a deep breath. "I need to go there, close the door on that part of my life. So I can move on."

I swallowed and nodded. The stay versus go debate wasn't even on the table.

He turned so he was facing me, and he rested a hand on my knee. "I'm hitting you where it hurts most, aren't I? I'm leaving with no warning when you were hoping I'd be here for you."

Like my father used to do. He didn't have to say it. It hung heavy in the air between us.

"Will you be here when I come back?"

I frowned. "You mean stay in your apartment while you're away?"

He nodded. "I have to try. This morning I got the feeling I might not have much time." He brushed a curly lock off my face. "Stay here. Sleep, walk around in the snow, buy all the Christmas crap they sell around here. And when things get bad, I'll think about you here at my table, sitting next to me like it's the most natural thing in the world."

I swallowed. I had spent my life quashing hopes in the face of reality. But with Jonas, I had thought that maybe, just this once, I wouldn't have to. That maybe some of my hopes could come true. Instead, I'd be waiting in an empty apartment for him to come home. Or flying back to my own empty New York apartment. Another test of our tenuous relationship, so soon.

"I don't know," I whispered.

He nodded and looked away. He rubbed the scruff of his jaw slowly.

"That's fair," he finally said. "I won't push you."

I stood up slowly. I had never sat on a man's lap or even wanted to. But today, I wrapped my arms around Jonas's neck and sat down on his thick, muscular thighs. His arms closed around me, and he buried his head in my neck and squeezed tighter.

4

I BLINKED OPEN my eyes at the rays of hazy light streaming through the window. I was here in Stockholm, sleeping in Jonas's bed. Without him.

To stay or to go? I definitely wasn't ready to do much of anything yet.

I had been half-awake when he left. We had stayed up long into the night, talking, kissing, dozing off. In the darkness of the morning, he settled behind me and teased my legs open one more time. Whispered how much he wanted me. How much he needed me. How he couldn't bring himself to leave me.

But he did. And I must have slept through his last kiss goodbye. Now it was so quiet in this little room, and the pillow smelled like Jonas. I could spend all day like this. Or maybe I already had.

I sat up and rubbed my eyes. Snow fell on the window sill, glowing in the sunlight. What time was it?

There weren't a lot of light hours in Stockholm in December, so it had to be near the middle of the day.

I rolled out of bed and headed for the kitchen. The clock on the oven read 12:56. I had slept half the day away. Probably good, but what the hell was I supposed to do with the rest of the holiday alone in Jonas's apartment?

I couldn't call my mother, who had warned a dozen times that coming to Stockholm for Christmas was setting myself up for disappointment. *I told you so* was already echoing loudly enough in my ears without my mother's words adding to the chorus. I had even left out the part when he told me not to come.

The counter was mostly bare except for the same envelope with my name on it that I had seen the day before. Next to it was a new note in Jonas's messy handwriting, folded up so that only the words *Dear Alice* showed at the top. I picked up the envelope first and held it to the light. Nothing decipherable.

I could open it. It was Christmas Day, after all, and there were no other presents in sight. But maybe it was better to decide whether I was staying before I peeked.

Instead, I grabbed the other note and sank into one of his dining chairs, placing the paper in front of me.

Another letter, probably just telling me about the emergency exits. But still a letter. Back in New York I had read each one he sent dozens of times.

I unfolded the paper. Tucked inside was a hand-drawn map of the neighborhood with the grocery store, a bank machine and the pharmacy labelled. On the side of the map, he wrote a few phone numbers, including for the ambulance and a pizza delivery place. There was some Swedish money, too, just in case, he wrote.

But the letter itself was different. Most of it was a description of me as I slept that morning. How it felt to sit next to me, memorizing all the details he had forgotten these last months, in case I was gone when he returned.

The letter ended with coffee pot instructions and a run-down of my breakfast options. Slim pickings. More sandwiches like we had eaten the night before or cereal and milk.

Sorry. Wasn't really expecting company. Was this line a jab or just the truth?

I fiddled with the coffee pot and turned it on. While I waited, I wandered around the kitchen, opening drawers and cabinets to study the contents, looking for… what was I looking for? Clues? There was so little in this apartment. Each object was chosen for a reason.

Most of the drawers were pretty bare, with a few ordinary things like silverware and scissors. But in the last one I found a stack of newspaper articles about Jonas. They were in all different languages, but each used the same photo of him, tattoos and muscles peeking out of a white t-shirt, hands shoved in his jeans, and those intense eyes, with no trace of a smile.

I picked out the English ones and read each carefully, looking for clues. But they were about the man who had sat across from me at the Boars and Allen conference room table, scowling. Not what I was looking for.

Above the fridge, in the cabinets I could barely reach, I found the biggest surprise. Candy. Lots of it. Chocolate bars, licorice, bags of assorted bulk candies of all kinds. Jonas had a sweet tooth? I wouldn't have guessed it. He was the opposite of indulgence, the model of self-control. And he kept a giant stash of candy? I pictured him standing where I was, eating one of the chocolate bars in two enormous bites, and chuckled.

After a few sips of coffee, I returned to his bedroom, ready to take myself on a real tour. Standing in front of his open closet, I inspected the shirts, taking in the ones he chose, imagining what each would look like as he pulled it over his bare chest. The scent of him lingered on everything, so I slipped one on and fastened a few of the buttons. I pulled out the one suit he owned and inspected it. Nicely made. Where did he wear it?

I closed the wardrobe doors and headed down the hall to the living room. I wandered across the bare wooden floor to browse his bookshelf. Most of the titles were in Swedish, but I recognized a few names.

At the end was his desk. I pulled out the ultra-modern chair and sat down. Surprisingly comfortable. I had found the first place where Jonas spent the money that must be pouring in, now that he had sold the movie rights to his first three books.

I rested my elbows on the old desk. What was it like to be Jonas in this silent apartment as he wrote? I glanced down at the rows of drawers on either side. Did I open them? It was his writing desk, not his diary, right? And he hadn't told me not to look around. Not that I had given him much chance to think of this possibility.

I frowned. Just a peek. I'd stop if I found anything private.

The top right drawer held pencils, pens, erasers, paperclips, and other miscellaneous office gadgets. And a post card of the Eiffel Tower. I flipped it over, but no one had written on it. The next one down was filled with blank loose leaf paper. The third was filled with bundles of papers, the pages filled with Jonas's writing. Everything was in Swedish, saving me from the decision of snooping or not. The row of drawers was exactly like his apartment. Bare, anonymous.

The top left drawer was filled with contracts and other business papers, some in English, some in Swedish.

I tugged open the next drawer down, slowing as I pulled it out. This one wasn't anonymous. There was a little stack of photos, most of them older, worn. In one, a group of boys stood in front of a run-down apartment building. Maybe *Norr*, the area where he grew up? I squinted, studying the boys, until I found him. Jonas was on the end, already taller than the rest of them, already with that *don't fuck with me* look on his face. They all had some version of that look, but Jonas was the one who had mastered it.

I slowly leafed through more childhood photos until I came to one that made me stop. The photo captured Jonas, a man and a woman at a picnic table. All three of them were making attempts at smiles, and no one succeeded. The man looked almost exactly like Jonas. Thinner, a little older, a lot more worn, but the similarity was striking. His father. I studied the photo for a while before I slipped it back into the pile.

Taking a deep breath, I opened the last drawer. More photos, no longer of Jonas's childhood. The top one was of him, together with three other guys, sitting around a pub table full of beers. The guys all sported tattoos and one was bandaged above the eye, but they were all smiling. I furrowed my brow as I studied the expression on Jonas's face. He was smiling, really smiling. It wasn't just the fighting he had left behind when he got out of prison. He had never once mentioned friends in his letters. I swallowed back a lump in my throat. Jonas must be so lonely.

There were more photos of his life before prison. One looked like it was just before a fight. He was shirtless, knuckles taped, mouth guard in hand, and he had the sexiest smirk on his face. A rush of liquid pleasure ran through me. I took the photo out of the pile and set it on his desk, then continued sifting through.

Until I came to one that took my breath away. Jonas, in front of the Eiffel Tower, with his arm draped around a woman with red hair. His Irish ex-girlfriend. The woman was a lot prettier than me, with high, prominent cheekbones and a haughty smile, and she didn't seem to mind the untamed look of her curly red hair.

Jonas had saved a photo of them together. Had he saved anything else? My hands shook as I set down the pile of photos and opened the drawer further. And there they were. A bundle of letters, sent from Siobhan Dillon in Dublin, Ireland.

I took out the little stack and set it on his desk, next to the photo of him. I stared at the envelopes, biting my lip. Siobhan was Irish, so the letters would be in English. And here they were, for me to read. Well, not quite. But in those envelopes could be the answers to the questions that I kept coming back to. Who was the woman who walked down the path of self-destruction next to him? Did he still fight the urge to go back to her?

Who wouldn't want a woman with a name like Siobhan?

These questions were the kind of crazy thoughts I had promised myself I'd never, ever let myself ask. I wasn't the kind of woman who secretly read my boyfriend's private letters, was I? I let out a sigh of irritation. Was Jonas even my boyfriend? That word was so frivolous, unnuanced.

I brushed my fingers over his name. Whether or not I opened these letters, I was that kind of crazy over Jonas. Which meant I wasn't leaving yet.

I picked up the photo of Jonas once more as he smirked back up at me. Of all the men in the world, it had to be this one? I set the photo on the sack of letters and stood up. I needed a little more coffee first if I was going to pry into his life.

JONAS CALLED ON the second day as I was lying in bed, his voice tense.

"You still at my place?"

"Your chocolate supply hasn't run out yet."

Jonas let out what sounded like a sigh of relief, mixed with a laugh. "Oh, right. You found all that?"

"And more," I said. "You've given me plenty of time to snoop."

"I probably have the world's least interesting apartment to explore," he said, amused.

"I don't know about that," I said. "Some of those sex toys are pretty interesting."

Jonas snorted. "You must have been looking in your own bag. I prefer my hand."

I laughed, but my cheeks flushed at the image of him getting himself off, right where I lay. What did he think about when he used his hand? I had all day to imagine it.

We had talked on the phone before, but it never felt like this. So close, so intimate. I was in his bed, surrounded by his life. Did the opposite of lonely have a name?

The line had been quiet for a while.

"How are things with your father so far?" I asked.

"Not good," he said. "He's mad that I helped my mother move out, mad that the neighbors make noise, mad at the store for raising the price of beer." He sighed. "I don't think he knows any other way to be."

His voice broke a little as he spoke.

"Are you okay, Jonas?" I asked.

"I'm a lot better right now, just talking to you."

IT WAS IMPOSSIBLE to escape Christmas in Stockholm. The holiday spirit was everywhere. Warm, cozy little scenes set up in the windows of every shop and apartment. Even the fire station I wandered past had candles in the windows.

I was sorely tempted to buy something cheerful to keep my company in Jonas's bare apartment. But wandering through these streets, thinking about his Christmas story, I was finally starting to understand his aversion to the holiday spirit. It was a constant, nagging reminder, wherever he turned, of the kind of warmth he had missed his whole life.

But he didn't have to resort to his prison-like décor, did he? If I was going to make it through these last days without him, I needed to do something about it.

Rounding the icy corner back home, I slowed by the flower shop window. Green. In the middle of all the grey and white of the winter day, the bright green called to me. This is what Jonas needed. Plants.

The door jingled as I entered, and I let down my hunched shoulders in the warm, humid air. There was so much to look at. Bouquets of flowers, tall leafy plants, ferns, mossy arrangements in fancy pots. The place was a miniature jungle, lit by strings of tiny white lights. There were a few Christmas-y bows around the pots, but mostly it was just green.

The woman at the counter said a few words to me.

"Do you speak English?" I asked.

The woman nodded.

So many plants to choose from, and I only had two hands to carry them back to the apartment. I pointed to a blue glazed pot with flowers and moss spilling over the edges.

"I'd like this one, please," I said. "And do you sell the strings of lights, too?"

I SAT DOWN at Jonas's desk, the pile of temptation in front of me. I stared at the collection of envelopes, making up my own versions in my head. Flirty Siobhan who writes dirty letters. Talkative, affectionate Siobhan who misses Jonas. Why the hell did he keep them?

But even worse was the fact that I hadn't sent him one single letter these last months. I had started many, and they all came out boring and impersonal. But not

Siobhan. She wrote a whole pile of them, good enough for Jonas to keep.

If Jonas walked in right now and saw me holding his letters, would he look at me with the same hot, dark stare from Christmas Eve, a dangerous mix of angry and turned on? Sitting at his desk, eating his candy, sleeping in his bed – I was in the middle of some sort of erotic Goldilocks tale. Up against the wall, his heavy body pressing into mine, his voice rough in my ear.

Who's been reading my letters?

I buried my face in my hands and shook my head slowly. I really needed to get out of this apartment. Jonas definitely needed another plant or two.

5

HE RETURNED SOMEWHERE in the deep of the night. I woke up to the heat of his body behind me, his breath in my hair. Jonas's hands caressed my stomach in soft strokes.

I turned around and brushed my hand over his cheek, a few days of stubble under my fingertips. His face was lit by the string of tiny lights I had hung in his window. He smiled a little, and his eyes were full of warmth.

"Hey," I whispered.

Jonas laughed softly. "Did I wake you?"

I rolled my eyes. "I'm sure you didn't mean to."

His hand skimmed over my shoulder, and he kissed me.

"Nice plants," he said.

"You like them? I wasn't sure."

He chuckled. "Looks like you were pretty sure. They're everywhere."

Okay, so maybe I had gone a little overboard, but once I started, it was hard to stop. Cut flowers for the table, a spiny cactus for his desk, an enormous fern for the corner of the living room. But my favorite was the little mossy arrangement in a decorative pot on the bedroom windowsill.

"Is it too much?" I asked.

"Not at all. I can't tell you how good it felt to come home to this."

I had worn one of his t-shirts to bed, and he slipped his hands underneath, around my waist, and pulled my closer. His erection pressed hard against me.

"How long ago did you get in?"

"Maybe an hour ago."

"And you've just been lying here like... this?" I moved against his erection, and he groaned.

"Pretty much."

He stroked my cheek, my hair, my neck. "God, this feels good."

"Coming home to a half-naked woman in your bed?"

He smiled and kissed me. "Knowing you've been here while I was gone. I thought about it all the way home on the train ride."

"And all the things you wanted to do?"

"Some of that," he said. "Well, plenty of that. But more, too. What I wanted to tell you, what you'd say, what you ate while I was gone. Boring, everyday things."

I blinked up at him. His eyes were so serious.

"I ate a lot of scrambled eggs. And chocolate," I said. "I'm hoping for a change today."

He rolled over on top of me. He was so hard, pushing against me. I sighed and moved under him, finding new ways for our bodies to fit together. He held my face in his hands and kissed me.

"How's your dad?" I asked.

He frowned a little. "Not great."

"I'm glad you went."

"Me, too. Especially since you're still here." His fingers traced paths down my neck, over my shoulder. "I told him about you."

Interesting.

"What did you say?"

He rested higher on his elbows. His big, tattooed body covered mine, separated only by a flimsy t-shirt. Slowly he lowered his lips to mine for another soft kiss. When he raised his head again, his deep blue eyes were steady on mine.

"I told him I'm falling in love with someone. Someone different."

My heart stuttered. This was really happening. There had been more than enough time in between Paris and New York and now Stockholm, more than enough for the glow of excitement and sex to wear off. And still.

This man, with a god-like body and a terrible past and a tenderness that took me by surprise each time. This man. Need and want and that persistent giddiness all threatened to crash over me as Jonas moved over me.

"I think I'm already in love with you," I whispered. "More than I should be."

He stilled above me. "Even after that messed-up night on Christmas Eve?"

"I'm afraid so," I said, smiling a little.

His eyes brimmed with warmth and tenderness. He leaned down and kissed my neck, and I took a long inhale. God, this man smelled good.

I buried my face in his hair and whispered, "I kept myself busy this week."

Jonas looked up at me, his eyebrows raised, his eyes sparking in amusement. "Doing what?"

"Reading a bunch of articles about you, eating most of your candy, staring at letters from your ex-girlfriend." My voice quivered on the last words.

Jonas froze. "Letters from my ex-girlfriend?"

I nodded. "I didn't read them. But I wanted to."

"Why?"

"I wanted to know who this woman was that kept you hanging on. You must miss her if you kept her letters all these years." My voice was thin and wobbly.

"No." Jonas shook his head. He looked almost angry. "No, Alice. That's what you thought all week? That I kept the letters because I missed her?"

"Yes," I whispered. My heart was pounding so hard now. I bit my lip. How many times had I told myself I wouldn't get upset over this?

"You should have read them." He let out a hiss of frustration. "She wrote to ask me for money, Alice."

My eyes widened. That's what was in those letters that I had stared at all week? I blinked up at him.

"That's it? Why did you keep them?"

Jonas frowned. "It's hard to explain."

I gave him a pointed look. "Try."

He stroked my cheek and took a deep breath. "When I read them, I can remember what it felt like to be me at that time. And it wasn't good. Her letters are what convinced me to leave that whole life behind."

"Oh."

He brushed my hair off my face, his big palms so impossibly gentle. "Every time I'm tempted to do something really stupid, I read them."

I stared up into his stormy blue eyes and let out a shaky laugh. "That was my second guess."

He looked down at me, studying my face, his forehead creased. Then a slow smile grew, lighting up his face. "Sure it was."

He was so beautiful when he smiled. He kissed me, coaxing my lips open, exploring my mouth with long, hot strokes of his tongue. I wrapped my legs around him and flexed my hips against his.

"Fuck," he muttered. "You're in my bed, wearing my t-shirt, and you're so soft and warm."

I stroked my fingers over the muscles of his back. "This week I dreamed of waking up with you next to me, too."

"I want to get this right, Alice," he whispered. "New York was intense. And hot. But this is what I want. This."

"Right now, you're getting it exactly right," I said.

I closed my eyes and breathed in his warm scent. At this moment, everything *was* right. The hard muscles of his arms around me, his raspy breaths in my ear, his hard erection against my belly, a reminder of where this was going. And how good it would be.

I smiled up at him. "Let me get undressed."

Jonas sat back on his knees to watch, and I lifted off his old shirt and wriggled out of my panties. He was already naked, his heavy chest rising and falling with each breath. But his gaze didn't move down the curves of my body this time. His eyes met mine, and finally I recognized what I had seen glimpses of before. Happiness. Real happiness.

I smiled a little, and the corners of his mouth quirked up. He climbed over me again and rested between my legs. His gaze stayed fixed on mine as he lowered his body. His skin was hot, and his hard muscles flexed as I touched them.

"It was a lot to ask of you to wait here when I left, to just be here for me. Especially considering the way I was when you came." He brushed my hair off my face and stroked my cheek. "I can be there for you, too. If you'll let me."

Trust me, his eyes said. *See the real me.*

I swallowed the flood of emotions that threatened. "I want that, Jonas. I'm trying."

He blinked, and for a moment I thought I saw tears in his eyes. But he leaned down to kiss me before I was sure. This was everything I had wanted when I stood at his doorstep.

He rested on one elbow and glided his hand down my body, teasing, caressing. He closed his hand around his erection and stroked it before guiding himself to my entrance.

"I'm trying, too," he whispered. "I want you so, so much."

On his last word, he thrust deep inside. I gasped for air as my body adjusted. Everywhere we touched fit together perfectly. Jonas found my hands and laced our fingers together. He squeezed, and I squeezed back. His beautiful blue eyes shone with hope and wonder. *This is real. I'll love you the best way I know how.*

My heart ached as I answered silently. *You're what I want. You're what I've been missing all this time.*

His rhythm was slow and unhurried, reverent and heartbreakingly tender. He was giving me things I never hoped to have. Things I had tried so hard not to hope for. I wrapped my legs around his, bringing him closer, matching my hips with his. Over and over, he said with every move, *I'm falling in love with you. Please let me in.*

"Yes," I whispered. "Yes."

He groaned and gave a few hard thrusts, pushing me over the edge into ecstasy. He followed, biting out my name, holding me.

"I'M NOT SURE if the pub will be open tonight," said Jonas, kicking a chunk of snow off the sidewalk with his thick hiking boots. "New Year's Eve gets a little rowdy, and they might not want to deal with it."

I pulled my coat tighter against the cold.

"But it's where we met." I smiled up at him. "What's the matter? I thought you liked mushy and romantic."

The corners of his mouth turned up, and he shrugged. "I just want tonight to be good. And some of the assholes that hang around that place, on a night like tonight..."

Jonas shoved his hands in his pocket and shook his head. The soft glow of the streetlights lit his face, exaggerating his brooding frown. But I smiled at him, and slowly, he smiled back.

I tightened my hand around the envelope in my pocket. It was New Year's Eve. I was running out of time. Tonight was the night to give it to him.

We walked along the narrow sidewalk, the city noises muted by the blanket of snow that covered everything. Firecrackers echoed through the streets, some close, some far away.

"It's not midnight yet, is it?" I asked.

"Still a few hours left," he said. "People shoot off shit all night long."

I laughed. "Not a fan of New Year's Eve, either?"

Jonas smiled a little. "Just never really had anyone to celebrate with. Until now."

His smile grew, that smile he gave me when no one else was looking. When we shut the rest of the world out, when it was just the two of us.

"Your call." His eyes glittered. "I'd take you somewhere more romantic and squishy, but it might offend your refined New York tastes."

I rolled my eyes. "As fun as it is to walk in the cold while you harass me, I think I'm voting for the pub."

Jonas chuckled. The snow came down harder, covering his broad shoulders.

He took my hand and squeezed it. "Did you celebrate Christmas with your mom before you left?"

I nodded. "I haven't been to her place in years. My aunt moved in with her, so she and my cousins were there too. On a scale of family Christmases, it was pretty good."

Bits of snow came in over the tops of my boots, seeping through my extra socks. He stroked my hand with his thumb.

"Any good presents?"

"I got a clay figurine of a cat, made by my seven-year-old niece." And a gift certificate for a hair consultation and cut, a not-so-subtle self-improvement suggestion from my mother. "What about you, Mr. Grinch? Did you get anyone a present this year?"

Jonas shrugged.

"Maybe," he said, but he didn't elaborate.

We passed a familiar corner store.

"Hey look. It's our store, where you bought condoms that first night," I said, elbowing him. "How romantic."

The corners of his mouth turned up. "You looked happy to see them when I brought them out."

"Give me a minute," I said, ducking into the warm entrance.

I grabbed two candy bars from the counter and handed the man some Swedish bills I had stuffed in my pocket. Jonas was waiting on the sidewalk where I left him, hands in his pockets.

I handed the candy bars to him. "For the New Year's countdown. We can toast with these."

His smile lit up his face. He put the candy bars into his pocket and pulled me into his arms. His breath in my hair, he kissed the top of my head.

"Thank you," he whispered.

Groups of celebrators jostled around us on the snowy sidewalk, boisterous and seemingly oblivious to the cold, along with couples, more subdued. I caught a glimpse of a cute blond woman ogling Jonas.

I pulled back to peek up at Jonas, just to see his reaction, but he was staring down at me like there was nothing else in the world that mattered to him. His warm hand stroked my cheek. "Just promise me we'll leave the pub if it gets too rough."

"Don't worry," I said. "If anyone gets rough with you, I'll take care of them."

He tipped his head back and smiled into the snowy sky. A real smile. He shook his head and found my hand.

"I'm not that good at doing regular couple things," he said. "But I'm willing to try if that's what you want."

"Thank you," I whispered. How had I never realized just how badly I wanted that?

"You know, some twisted part of me is glad you came early," he said. "It's a relief, knowing you're still here even after I fucked up so badly."

I blinked up at him. He watched me for a while, brushing my hair over my shoulders. All the laughter from moments before was gone.

"But I hate that I was that way with you. I'm so, so sorry." His eyes were serious and sad.

"It's okay," I said. It really was. "You were right that day. I think some twisted part of me needed to know, too."

Jonas nodded a little and squeezed my hand.

I clenched the envelope in my pocket with my other hand. My heart gave a little jolt. Before we left, he had watched me as I picked it up out of my bag. Then he ducked into the kitchen and came out with his own envelope, the one that had been waiting there all week.

We rounded the slushy corner, and Jonas held the door open for me. The place was as dimly lit as the Stockholm sidewalks, with groups of people, mostly men, clustered around the bar, talking loudly. Just a few steps away, a man with carefully gelled hair took a shot and stumbled back toward me. Jonas wrapped his arm around my shoulder and pulled me closer.

"Looks like a promising night," I said.

"Your idea, not mine," he said dryly.

"But it's where we met."

Jonas gave an exasperated sigh. "We could get that hotel room from the first night. Spend some time there instead."

I smiled up at him. "Come on. It'll be fine."

The booth where we first had sat together was empty. I tugged on his hand, and he followed me across the pub. Heads turned as we passed the bar, straight out of a bad movie. I slid into the booth. Jonas unzipped his coat and tossed it on the opposite bench.

"What do you want to drink?" he asked.

I frowned. Right. We were in a bar, and he didn't drink... except when he really did. Maybe coming here was a bad idea.

"We don't have to stay here," I said quickly, moving to the edge.

Jonas raised his eyebrows. He rested one hand on the back of the booth and the other on the table, leaning over me.

"Are you afraid I'm going to order a half bottle of whiskey?"

I couldn't tell if he was joking or not.

"I guess not," I said slowly.

Jonas shrugged. "I eat here with my mother every Sunday, remember?"

I nodded slowly. "Okay. Then surprise me. Bring me anything."

"Except beer, right?" he said, cracking a smile. "You're the American who doesn't like beer."

"Right."

Jonas headed for the bar, and I watched him as he crossed the room. He was an impressive man by any standards, tall, clearly fit, even under the winter layers. The huddled groups parted as he neared. He leaned in to talk to the bartender, giving me a view of the perfect fit of his jeans. My cheeks flushed. I glanced around, but no one was paying attention.

I pulled the crumpled envelope from my pocket and set it on the table, smoothing it out. Jonas returned with a glass of champagne and a soda. He slid in close, just as he had the first night we met. His gaze rested on the envelope I had set out. He slipped one hand onto my thigh and raised his glass to me.

"To a new year. A new start."

"A new start," I echoed.

I drank a sip of champagne and set it down. It was time. I took a deep breath and picked up the thick envelope, with his name in neat letters. I bit my lip and handed it to him. He opened it, unfolding the pages, one by one. He stared down at the very first letter. My heart pounded. And I waited. Too many minutes passed as he slowly turned the pages.

Finally, he looked up, his eyes wide.

"These are letters to me?"

"They're nothing like yours," I said quickly. "And I quit part way through most of them. It's stuff I'm not used to talking about. But I really wanted to try, and I finished a couple on the plane ride over."

My voice died out. He was looking at the pages again, and I turned away. This was probably a bad idea.

"Sorry," I said. "They're a bit of a downer. You were probably expecting something—"

"Alice?" Jonas rested his hand on my cheek, gently turning my face toward his. "There's nothing in the world that I would want more. Thank you."

"It might not be very interesting," I mumbled. "I was trying to be honest with you. Like you were in your letters."

"Thank you," he said again.

Her face must have been bright red at this point. He tugged on the zipper of my coat until it opened at the top. He slipped his hand behind my neck and stroked me with his thumb. "Do you want me to read them after you leave?"

I nodded.

"Okay. Then it's time for my gift." He pulled the envelope out of his pocket, the one I had seen the first day in the kitchen. "I'm impressed you didn't open it while I was gone."

I rolled my eyes. "You're looking at years of experience at self-denial. I'm a pro."

Actually, if I hadn't been distracted by Siobhan Dillon's letters all week, I probably would have peeked.

"This gift isn't nearly as personal as yours," he said, rubbing the back of his neck.

His cheeks flushed, and he frowned a little. Was Jonas nervous? I had never seen him this way before.

I rested my hand on his arm. "I might not like it?"

Jonas shook his head. "Not that. It might scare you off."

I furrowed my brow. What would fit in an envelope and also scare me off? The court papers from his prison sentence? That would be a pretty morbid present, even for Jonas.

His pulse ticked quickly at the base of his throat, and he swallowed as he handed it to me. The envelope was warm, and I stared down at it, trying not to tear it open. His last gift, the earrings, had hit me hard. I needed to be ready for whatever this was.

"Go ahead," he whispered. "Open it."

I opened the envelope and pulled out a single sheet of paper. My hands trembled as I unfolded it. On it was a photo of a house right on the water, with a dock and a rocky shore. Pine trees in the background.

I looked up at him, brow furrowed. "It's a nice photo," I said weakly. "Did you take it?"

"I did," he said cautiously. "But do you like that place?"

"I do," I said slowly. "What is it?"

Jonas rubbed the back of his neck and looked away. "Well, I bought it. For us."

"What?" My voice came out in a loud squawk. "You just went out and bought a house for us? Without even knowing if I'd come?"

I rubbed my forehead. Whoa.

Jonas took a deep breath. "Look, I spent a lot of time this fall trying to figure out what to do. I want to be with you. I want to have what we had in Paris together, but for real this time."

I swallowed.

"But I'm so afraid I'm going to fuck it all up when we're here, right in the middle of my life. When I saw the listing for this place, far out in the Stockholm archipelago, I knew it would be perfect. I want it to be just the two of us."

"So you bought... a house?" I asked slowly, almost to myself.

"You look a little mad about it," he said.

I let out a gulp of a laugh and shook my head. "I don't know what I feel. It's a lot to take in."

"This is what I want. I'm all in."

I shook my head slowly. "This isn't how people usually do it, Jonas. We're missing some in between steps. Most people don't buy a house until after they're married."

Jonas wrinkled his brow. "I don't want to get married unless we're really, really sure."

He looked like he was actually considering it.

My stomach was doing flips. I rubbed my temples. "I have a job."

"So quit it. Say goodbye to that asshole ex-boyfriend of yours forever."

"We don't even know each other very well," I whispered.

He nodded slowly. "That's why we go to this place in the summer. Just us, nothing else. We learn what it's like to be together, have something more. Something that could last."

I took a shaky breath. This was it. My biggest fear was about to be voiced aloud in a noisy pub in Stockholm for the whole world to hear.

I looked down at the beautiful house one more time. "But what happens when I'm no longer the thing you're into? What happens when you get tired of us?"

What if you see more of the real me, and you change your mind?

Jonas shook his head. "No," he said gruffly. "That's not going to happen."

He clenched his fists and let out a huff of a breath. Then he turned to me. Slowly, he pulled the zipper of my coat the rest of the way down. He slipped his hand inside, around my waist. The heat of his palm soaked through my shirt as he stroked gently, up and down. He pulled me close, and I buried my face in his chest. I took a deep breath, blocking out everything else but him.

"There are no guarantees, Alice," he said, his voice rumbling from deep inside. "It's possible I'll hurt you in all the ways you're most scared of. But in the end, you have to decide if you trust what we have between us. If that's what you want."

"And we just wait until the summer for it?" I whispered, closing my eyes.

"I've been waiting my whole life to feel this way," he said. "You tell me you're coming, and I can wait as long as I have to."

A cheer echoed through the pub. The place was getting louder and a little rowdier. I straightened up.

"This isn't just one more night anymore," he said softly. "You know that, don't you?"

I laughed. "It's more than a week this time. Unless you're planning to kick me out tomorrow."

Jonas shook his head. "That's not what I mean."

"I know." I took a deep breath, and my lip quivered.

His eyes were dark, and he held my gaze.

"My past isn't going away, Alice," he said. "But I'm tired of being scared of it. I want this future with you more. You and me." His large hands explored higher, under the swells of my breasts. "I want to know that you're all in, too."

Another round of cheers erupted from the bar. I glanced at my watch.

"Only a few minutes until midnight," I said.

He nodded.

"What do you say, Alice?"

The people around us were chanting in Swedish now, probably counting down. A new year. A new start. And I wanted that new start to be with him. More than anything.

"I'm all in, Jonas," I said. "I'll come this summer, and if it goes well..."

"No ifs, Alice," he said. "This is where we start for real."

Cheers and horns rang out through the tiny pub, and firecrackers exploded everywhere outside. He pulled a candy bar out of his pocket and peeled off the wrapper.

"Happy New Year, Alice," said Jonas, raising the squares of dark chocolate to my mouth.

"A new start," I repeated softly.

I took a bite of his rich, smooth candy bar, my gaze fixed on Jonas's intense blue eyes, blazing with the kind of happiness I had waited for my whole life. Yes, this man would love me. And I would love him back. So simple, but it was everything.

He took a bite and set the chocolate on the table. Smiling, I cupped his face in my hands. I brought my lips to his, but I didn't close my eyes. I stared at him up close as he watched me, patiently waiting.

"This is it," I whispered against his lips. "The beginning of us."

EPILOGUE

JONAS SLOWED THE boat as we neared the cove of the tiny island, sending a cascade of ripples out in all directions. I touched my hair, feeling out the scale of disaster after the windy ride. Ugh. Hopeless.

The sleepy little island was mostly pine trees and rock, with a few cabins peeking out at the shore, most painted bright red with white trim. Except the one we were headed toward. The bigger, modern creation on the shore came into view. I stood up, holding onto the bow window to steady myself.

It was real. The summer house wasn't just an insane dream I had last New Year's Eve. The little island in the Stockholm archipelago, the July sun warming my back, and the man standing next to me – all real.

Jonas had spent most of June getting the place ready. His letters had detailed projects like repairing the boat mooring and building a new deck across the rocks, and the effects on him were clear. His hair had bleached light blond, and his skin was golden. Not just his arms. I had gotten a peek under his shirt as he lifted the bags into the boat, and his stomach was just as deliciously sun-kissed.

He must have been working outside without a shirt all month. If I had exposed myself to the sun for that long, my skin would be a shocking beet red by now. Not his. I had already pictured the scene a dozen times since we pushed off the Stockholm dock. Jonas, shirtless in jeans, lifting a pile of wooden planks, his tattoos glistening with sweat—

"This is it," said Jonas over the noise of the motor, cutting into my fantasy world.

My heart thumped hard as we approached the narrow dock. It had a little ladder into the water, for swimming, presumably, and the newly built walkway connected it to the steps to the deck. Above that stood a house far bigger than any place I'd ever lived.

"It's beautiful, Jonas," I said.

He nodded. "It's quiet around here. I think an older poet owns the place next door, but I've never seen him."

He pointed to the little red cabin, small and unassuming next to the big, modern house. Jonas and my summer house. Far away from everything.

"I still can't believe you bought this place," I said as Jonas tied up the boat.

He pointed to the bags stowed under the deck, and I handed them to him, one by one. When the boat was emptied, he helped me out. As I stepped onto the dock, he pulled me in close, against the warmth of his body.

"I still can't believe you came," he said, letting a kiss linger on my lips. "I can't believe my crazy plan to be with you worked out."

"I've never been somewhere like this." It was the kind of place people with money owned. This was the kind of thing I had never even thought to want. It was so, so far out of reach for a girl from Brooklyn. And yet, there I was. With Jonas.

"Just tell me if the quiet starts to drive you crazy," he said.

"And then you'll buy us another place in the city?"

Jonas laughed. "If that's what you want."

He let me go and picked up the cooler. I grabbed my suitcase and followed him up toward the house. I rolled my little bag along the new walkway that winded through the rock and bumped it up the narrow steps to the deck. I stopped at the top and turned around. Jonas's boat floated peacefully next to the dock.

"Is the water cold here?" I asked, turning to him.

Jonas shrugged. "Not bad. Why? You want to swim?"

"No way," I said, shaking my head. "I don't know what's in that water."

He chuckled and gave my shoulder a squeeze. "I sense a new project on the horizon."

Two French doors opened up into a living room with high ceilings, almost bare aside from a long, grey couch, facing the water. The room flowed into the kitchen, also open, with a table and two chairs in the corner. In the middle of the counter was an enormous fern.

Jonas set down the cooler and watched me, rubbing his jaw. "It's a little bare. I thought you'd like the plant."

"I love it," I said, my voice shaky.

He nodded a little. "Let me put the groceries into the fridge, and then I'll show you the rest of the place."

Abandoning my suitcase in the doorway, I headed for the couch. I propped up the pillows at the end and leaned back to watch him. Jonas squatted down next to the cooler, lifting, rearranging, giving me glimpses of the muscles under his shirt. He glanced over his shoulder, catching my stare, but I didn't turn away. He smirked a little and went back to work.

"How did you get the money for a place like this?" I asked. "Writing books doesn't bring in that much, does it?"

Jonas shrugged. "International translations, the rights to make my whole series into movies. It brings in more than enough for a while."

I wrinkled my brow.

"I know it looks extravagant, but it really wasn't so much. This place isn't for everyone. It's a little deserted out here on this island. Many people would see that as a downside."

When he finished unpacking the cooler, he headed for the couch and sat down on the edge, next to me, so I had to move over. He turned and stroked my cheek. "I bought this place to give us the best possible shot at being together. That's what it is. A place where we have a chance."

"It's amazing," I whispered. "I've never been anywhere like this before."

He stroked my arm slowly, his long fingers curling around me, caressing. "Ready for the tour?"

I covered his hand with mine. "I have a bit of news, first."

He squeezed my arm, and his forehead creased. "Good or bad?"

"Good, I think," I said. "It's about work."

He raised his eyebrows. "Did you quit?"

"Sort-of."

He continued to caress my arm, his hand warm and heavy against my skin, waiting.

"I'm going to work as a freelance editor instead," I said. "Still with Boars and Allen, but I don't need to be at the office anymore."

Understanding registered in his eyes, and the wrinkles disappeared from his brow. "So you could work from here?"

I nodded. "If neither of us want to strangle the other after two weeks."

"Wow." He rubbed his other hand over his eyes.

"That's the good kind of wow, right?" I asked.

He met my gaze, his dark blue eyes warm. "The very best kind."

He brushed his lips against mine and gave my arm a last squeeze before letting it go.

"Come on," he said, standing up. "Let me show you around."

Jonas grabbed my bag and held out his hand. We peeked into his office and a bathroom before heading upstairs.

He pointed into an empty room to the left. "Your office, if you want."

I poked my head in. The room was probably as big as my apartment back in New York.

"This alone is worth not strangling you," I said.

Jonas smiled and nodded toward the other side of the staircase. "And the bedroom."

Like the rest of the house, the room was painted all white, with high ceilings, and most of the wall facing the water was covered with windows. A pair of French doors led out to a little balcony with two wooden chairs. In the middle of the room was a king-sized bed, covered with an enormous red comforter, with more than enough pillows piled at the head. Next to the bed were matching white bedside tables. Books were stacked on one, and a vase of red roses stood on the other.

I took a couple deep breaths and walked over to the closet, opening the doors. On one side, a few of Jonas's shirts hung on hangers, and the rest of his clothes were neatly folded on the shelves. The other side was bare.

I was the missing half of this room. He was waiting for me.

Jonas set down my suitcase in front of the closet and came up behind me. His hands slipped around my waist, moving up and down my sides in slow strokes.

"You can change anything you want," he said, his voice huskier.

I swallowed and shook my head. "No. It's perfect."

"It is now that you're here," he whispered. He moved my hair off my neck and pressed his lips onto my skin.

"Wait."

I freed myself from his hold and reached for my suitcase. Unzipping the front pocket, I pulled out a bundle of letters. He looked from the letters back to me.

I smiled. "They're yours. I want you to read them aloud to me."

Jonas raised an eyebrow at me.

"The good parts," I added.

He laughed. "You know where that's going to lead."

"To more good things." I walked over to the nightstand and set the letters next to the roses. I smiled at him over my shoulder. "I brought you some candy, too, if that's what you're in the mood for."

He shook his head and followed me over to the bed.

I took a deep breath. "When I read your letters, all I could think about was your voice."

I pulled out one from the pile and unfolded it. I skimmed the first side and flipped it over. "Here's one."

He looked over my shoulder to where I pointed. "We're starting with that?"

His blue eyes blazed with heat, and he sat down on the bed. He rolled onto his back and propped his head on a pillow. I faced him on my side, tangling our feet. No one on earth smelled as good as Jonas did. Slipping my hand under his t-shirt, I explored the relief of hard stomach muscles and golden blond tufts of hair.

"Ready when you are," I said.

After one more sideways glance at me, he cleared his throat and began to read.

"'Have I told you how often I dream of you? I probably have, but I'll tell you again.'" His voice was low and rough. "'We can be anywhere. Paris. New York. Even places we've never been together before. The Stockholm archipelago in the middle of the summer. It's beautiful there, by the way.'"

His eyes darted to mine, and he smiled.

"'Sometimes I have the loneliest kinds of dreams, where you say you'll be right back and disappear and I never find you. But more often, they're the other kind.'"

Jonas paused again, his eyes on me for an extra beat. I propped myself on my elbow and brushed my lips against his.

"Keep going," I said.

"'The kind that I wake up hard from.'" He let out a quiet groan and continued. "'Last night I had one of those. We were at the place I bought for us. You were in the water, and I was on the dock. No one else was around.'"

I stroked his stomach in slow circles. His breath hitched.

"'You climbed out, and you weren't wearing anything. All wet, your beautiful hair dripping down over your breasts. Just looking at me like I was the only thing in the world you wanted.'"

My hand brushed lower, and he groaned.

"What happened next?" I whispered.

"'You walked up and knelt between my legs.'" His voice was strained.

I got up on my hands and knees and climbed between his legs. His t-shirt rode up at the waist, hinting at the planes of sculpted muscles and tattoos across his body. This was too good to be true, but here we were, in the middle of the Stockholm archipelago, taking our first tentative steps together.

A bubble of warmth rose inside me. Finally, all my longing and waiting had a place.

"And then?" I asked, my voice shaking.

Jonas let out a strangled laugh and dropped the letter onto the floor. "Then I stopped reading and moved on to the real thing."

In an instant, I was on my back, and he was over me, propped up on his elbows.

"My turn to torture you," he mumbled, kissing my neck.

Jonas brushed my hair off my shoulder, over to one side. His rough fingers traced my collarbone, and he kissed my bare shoulder. His erection throbbed against me, but his kisses were soft and slow. His hands skimmed up and down, exploring, remembering. His breaths filled my ear, together with whispers of all the things he missed about me, all the things he wanted to do to me.

"Wait," I said, laughing. "What about the letters?"

"We have time for that, too. So much time."

It was true. We had forever. At last.

***

ABOUT THE AUTHOR

Rebecca Hunter is a writer and translator who has always loved to read and travel. Though she earned a Bachelor's in English and a Master's in English Education, most of what she learned about writing romance has come from other sources.

She has, over the years, called many places home, including Michigan, where she grew up, New York, San Francisco and, of course, Stockholm, Sweden. After their most recent move from Sweden back to the San Francisco Bay Area, she and her husband assured each other they'd never move again. Well, probably not.

Her debut book, *Stockholm Diaries, Caroline*, won the 2016 National Excellence in Romance Fiction Award (NERFA), and *Best Laid Plans*, her first book for the Harlequin DARE line, won the 2019 NERFA and the 2019 HOLT Medallion contests and earned a starred review from Library Journal. *Pure Satisfaction* won the VIVIAN Award in 2021.